Shh! It's a Secret:
a novel about Aliens, Hollywood, and the Bartender's Guide

by Daniel M. Kimmel

In-house editor: Ian Randal Strock

Fantastic Books
1380 East 17 Street, Suite 2233
Brooklyn, New York 11230
www.FantasticBooks.biz

ISBN 10: 1-61720-733-0
ISBN 13: 978-1-61720-733-4

First Edition

Dedicated with love and gratitude to my sister
Bonnie MacEntee, and it's about time.

"*A Trip to Mars* is a dignified, impressive, consistent propaganda spectacle, preaching peace and a better world on earth… There are no monsters or ogres, merely pure, simple-minded people who live cleanly and evidently in a mild climate that permits the wearing of filmy, flowing robes."

—movie review in *Variety*
July 18, 1919

Contents

Prologue
War of the Worlds

Look, I'm just a studio publicist. I don't know anything about being a diplomat except when to offer an exclusive behind-the-scenes cover story to *Vanity Fair* and when to offer it to *Entertainment Weekly*. It was never my intention to do anything that would set off an intergalactic war.

Yes, I know that's the wrong word. It's more like "interstellar" or "intersystem" but, damn it, I'm a flack, not an astronomer. All I was supposed to do was handle the film's gala premiere and our star. Our big opening night was supposed to be the end of the whole project, not the beginning.

And, really, what is the big deal? Do you know? It's a *positive* film. We *like* them. It's all about friendship and reconciliation between our two races, and how everyone in the universe is one big happy family. Geez, it was so non-controversial, even the Tea Party protestors should have liked it. Did you see it?

Now why should I have ever suspected that anything was going to go wrong? Abe never gave us a clue that there was a problem. That was another one of my jobs, you know, keeping him happy. I was pretty good at it, too, because I really like the guy. I made sure all his needs were taken care of, whether it was entertainment, or food, or privacy. He used to spend hours watching old sci-fi movies, and I made sure he had whatever he wanted.

What? The movies? No, I'm sure it wasn't that. I made it clear to him that it was all just Hollywood fantasy. Hell, some of those movies were older than me. Abe didn't care. He seemed to enjoy them.

Like I said, we became pals. I even invited him into my home to meet my wife and kids. He really hit it off with my older daughter. Do you know how hard it is to convince a five-year-old that she can't tell everyone on the block that her new best friend is from another planet? Really.

I think my actions have been beyond reproach, on behalf of the studio, the industry, the US, and the whole damned planet. I was a regular "goodwill ambassador." I was even thinking of putting in for a raise, before all this happened. You ought to be giving me a medal instead of keeping me locked up here.

I really don't know why I have to tell this story again. I've already told it several times since you picked me up this morning, and it's not going to change. After all, those are the facts. I can't make up new facts, can I?

Well, you're right: I suppose I can if one of our stars gets picked up drunk with a hooker, but this wasn't like that. First of all, Abe is just a sweetheart, not like that at all. Actors usually don't get swelled heads until after the opening weekend of a hit movie, and we haven't made it past the first preview.

Second, he mostly stayed on the lot. That was part of the deal. He really wanted to do the movie, and we didn't want anyone to get wind of it until the premiere. It's a competitive thing. Remember when there were those competing Truman Capote movies? That's what we were trying to avoid. We wanted to be the first one out of the gate.

So until the night of the premiere—until *after* the premiere—we had no idea that there was going to be a problem. We were expecting acclaim, riches, and a lot of free publicity, plus I was hoping for a few weeks of vacation. You know, this is hard work. It may not look like it, but I probably work as hard as you do. Of course, I don't go to work armed.

Sorry, nothing personal. See what I mean about how I'm not cut out to be a diplomat?

So, look, all I'm saying is that I have no idea what went wrong. We operated under the best intentions, with malice toward none and liberty and justice for all. It's just a movie, for crying out loud.

All I know is that I'm not going to take the rap.

The Day the Earth Stood Still

"Hey, is someone going to let me get a hit off that baby?"

What is it with otherwise normal adults? Put them in a room with a new baby, and nearly everyone wants to take turns holding it… or, in this case, her. Larissa and I had just had our second child, another girl, and the family had been coming and going all afternoon to meet God's newest creation, baby Elizabeth.

The person confusing the baby with a bong was my cousin Norm who, childless himself, could be very personable with people of all ages, but who might quickly lose interest if you didn't share any of his exceedingly narrow range of interests. Most of the time he was happiest when he was with his colleagues at the Jet Propulsion Laboratory. Five minutes trying to engage Norm in conversation would lead the average person to ask why people always assume that rocket scientists are smarter than the rest of us. Like anyone else who's good at his job, Norm does very well in his own field. It's the outside world where he's sometimes at a loss. While Norm was explaining to my mother-in-law that he didn't actually want to hit my newborn daughter, my attention was elsewhere.

I was off to one side of the living room, by the TV. I suppose you'll be wanting all sorts of descriptive, flowery prose, like what material the couch was upholstered with, and the pattern on the wallpaper, and what the weather was like, but I save that stuff for the press releases. At home, I just want to get right to the point. You want to know what the living room looked like? It was a California tract home. You looked out the window and you saw palm trees. There was a big couch along one wall, where Norm had now decided that holding a wet baby on his knee was not as exciting as having a dry one. On either side of the couch there were some matching chairs. We had brought in the dining room chairs for extra seating. With my eyes closed, I couldn't even tell you what color the couch was. I'd guess brown, but I'm sure Larissa would insist it was tan or taupe or beige or "earth tone." You want to know what the room looked like? Pick up *Architectural Digest*. The guy in the corner watching the TV is me. That's what I was focusing on at the moment.

Well, half-focusing. I was watching CNN with one eye and my older daughter Susan with the other. Though it was a lazy Saturday afternoon, CNN was going to be running a feature story that I had helped coordinate about *The Ducklings' Space Adventure*. This was the latest of the "Duckling" series of family films from Graham Studios, where I was the senior vice president in charge of publicity and promotion.

"C'mon, Susie, don't you want to see the story about the new 'Ducklings' movie?"

My daughter looked at me as if I had suggested she put down her ice cream and take another helping of broccoli. "Not *them* again," she complained. "Didn't I see this one already?"

"No, that was *The Ducklings' Undersea Adventure*. That was last year."

"But it's just the same story on a rocket ship, isn't it, Daddy?"

Great. She's almost five years old, and she's not only a film critic, but she's a cynic to boot. I suppose it can't be helped. I took her to the set once to meet the Duckling family, and when she learned that they were all animatronic puppets run by a bunch of techies through a series of cables, she decided that such make believe was for "little kids." She told me she'd rather see "real" ducks—like Daffy and Donald. So much for the age of innocence.

"Jake? Do you have the set on?" This was Larissa. She enjoyed my tangential relationship to the movies, but she liked to keep it separate from our home life. After all, today we were supposed to be making way for Elizabeth, not the Ducklings.

"It's just the one story, dear, then I promise I'll turn it off."

"It's one of those baby movies about the ducks," sneered Susan. "Maybe Elizabeth wants to see it."

"Now that will be enough of that," I insisted.

I had had the set down low. I was planning on recording the story and checking it over later. If everyone would just let me do my job, I could be done in five minutes and out on the patio setting up the barbecue. I turned to Larissa and put my hands up in what I hoped was a supplicating fashion.

"They do their entertainment stories at the bottom of the hour," I said. "It's almost over."

On screen, the blonde anchor with the big hair—as opposed to the brunette with the big hair—was announcing their Hollywood segment.

"Everyone's favorite bird family is off on a flight of a different kind this summer. Nat Williams has this report…"

Papa Duckling, complete with handlebar mustache and glasses, was at the controls of the family spaceship when the screen suddenly went blank.

"We interrupt our regularly scheduled programming for this live news event," intoned the announcer.

Now this was odd. It was Saturday afternoon. CNN routinely breaks in with live coverage of presidential press conferences or the like because, after all, that's what a news channel is supposed to do. But it was the weekend. News wasn't supposed to happen on the weekend. I switched over to MSNBC to see if this was real news, or just someone in the control room trying to jazz up the newscast on a slow day.

"…and as you can see behind me, we have a confirmed report. Some sort of alien spacecraft *has* landed here on the golf course outside the old Concord Hotel in Monticello, New York, here in the Catskill Mountains."

"What?" Norm nearly tripped over Susan as he ran over to the set to turn up the sound. On screen was what looked like a large metal box on four legs, with a kind of round ball on top.

"What's wrong with the camera, Daddy?"

We had all noticed the same thing. There was something about the geometry of the ball that wasn't quite right. It seemed to keep shifting or turning or something. The image just wouldn't come into focus. The anchor back in the studio seemed to be having the same problem, because he asked the reporter why the camera was malfunctioning.

"The camera's working just fine. It appears to be the ship itself. I'm not sure if it's moving or what, but spectators who have been looking at it report getting headaches from trying to figure out what shape it is. I'm getting a little woozy myself."

All thoughts of the barbecue or "Duckling" movies evaporated in an instant. Suddenly, we were all crowded around the set, trying to understand what was happening. Only Elizabeth remained oblivious, deciding that now would be an excellent time to eat. At this tender age, babies are primarily concerned with taking it in or moving it out. Larissa smoothly opened her blouse to give the baby access to her midday snack. Usually, when breast-feeding in public, she draped a towel or something over her shoulder, in an attempt at discretion. Such was our interest in what was going on onscreen that, two hours later, she was holding the now sleeping baby with the buttons still undone.

"The ship appeared at 2:15 this afternoon, Eastern Daylight Time," said the reporter, which would have made it late morning our time. "It was first reported by Mr. Robert Aguilar, the chief of the fire department in Peekskill, New York, who was out on the golf course when it landed."

The scene cut to a pre-recorded interview with the obviously shocked fire chief, who was looking decidedly unofficial in his leisure clothes. "We were out on the back nine, and I had just let fly with a beautiful shot to the green, when one of the other guys suddenly ducked. My ball had come flying back. Since we were on the fairway, I looked to see what it had hit, and that's when we saw it."

"Did anyone come out, or attempt to communicate with you?"

"Buddy, I've got two medals for bravery for rescuing injured people in the middle of raging fires, but I'm not ashamed to tell you: I didn't stick around to find out."

As they cut back to the live shot of the spacecraft—"flying saucer" just didn't seem appropriate—I turned to Norm to ask him what he made of it. But he was already on his cell phone, trying to get through to the Jet Propulsion Laboratory.

"Are we being invaded?" asked Susan, sounding a lot more like a small child than the cynical critic of the Ducklings she had been just a few minutes ago.

"Well, it certainly looks like we're being visited," said Norm, slipping his phone back into his pocket, "but you've got to do more than just park your vehicle in an inconvenient spot for it to constitute an invasion."

"So what is it, Norm?" I asked.

"Don't know. And they don't know at JPL, either, but they want me to come in. I'll just have to take a rain check on those burgers." He kissed Larissa and the baby good-bye and was out the door, off to do rocket scientist stuff. The rest of us sat mesmerized in front of the set for the rest of the day. Details were sparse, but nobody could think of anything better to do.

*   *   *

It was the following morning when the hatch or door or whatever it was finally opened. The top had finally come to rest. Rather than seeming round, it now looked as square as the bottom part. As a portion of the wall slid up, creating what the reporters were telling us must be a doorway, I thanked my lucky stars that our movie wasn't opening until next weekend. I knew that at this point that nobody was going anywhere for any reason any place on the planet. If you were breathing, you were in front of your TV.

If this was what everybody assumed it was, what we were witnessing was going to be a historic turning point for humanity. It wouldn't do in years to come, when Elizabeth asked, "Where were you when we found out we weren't alone in the universe, Daddy?" if I had to tell her I was out getting the car washed, or had run to the supermarket to pick up some baby wipes.

The one exception to this lack of activity, naturally, was in the Catskills Mountains. After decades where the hotels had been shutting down, converting to condos, or selling off to Chasidic Jewish groups, suddenly the Catskills were alive with excitement. Suddenly, there wasn't a room to be had in all of Sullivan County. Such was the demand that in nearby South Fallsburgh, a canny developer had paid top dollar to acquire the old Raleigh Hotel on the spot, and transform it back into a hotel. When there weren't enough rooms ready, he started setting up cots in the lobby and in the old nightclub, all to be rented at resort hotel rates. Nobody was coming for the show or the amenities. There was only one show that counted: the big opening act on the golf course at the Concord.

By now, the government had shown up and tried to cordon off the area around the ship, but with two dozen American camera crews already there, and more pouring in from around the country and around the world, it was a lost cause. This was bigger than national security. If we were going to meet some super race of aliens, it was going to be live on international television. I only hoped that they wouldn't come out and announce that they had only stopped to ask for directions.

On screen, we could see that the door had opened up, but still no one appeared. Clearly, our visitors were being as cautious as we were. Just as no humans had tried to approach the ship, none of whoever was inside seemed to be in any rush to come out. Instead, we heard a voice that sounded like it was coming from a loudspeaker. It sounded surprisingly human.

"People of Earth, we bring you greetings. We come in peace. We have tested your atmosphere and found it safe. Our ambassador will now be exiting our ship. Please do not be alarmed. All your questions will be answered in due course. Again, we come in peace and friendship. This is a historic day for both our peoples."

My sense of awe was overwhelming. Whoever these guys were, however developed their spacefaring civilization turned out to be, clearly these were beings who recognized the importance of smooth advance publicity. I decided right then that I wanted to meet them. Maybe we could exchange a few professional tips.

And then he appeared. It was amazing. He was clearly a he, human in size and shape, two eyes, a nose, a mouth, four limbs that looked just like arms and legs. His clothing consisted of a dark jacket and slacks, and a lighter colored shirt. The cut wasn't like anything I'd ever seen before, especially the lapels on the pants, but the overall effect was decidedly human, or at least humanoid.

So here he was, the first non-Earthling—to the best of anyone's knowledge—to ever walk across a Catskills golf course, and it was up to Sue to ask the question that was on everybody's mind.

"Daddy? Why is he blue?"

Altered States

Even with everyone moving at top speed, it still took forty-eight hours to arrange the special session of the United Nations General Assembly. Many, if not most, of the world's leaders chose to head their delegations, requiring additional seating not only for the enlarged delegations, but for the exponentially expanded press corps. After all, this wasn't Khrushchev with his shoe, or Arafat packing a gun. This was an honest-to-goodness space alien who wanted to address "the people of Earth." Part of the problem was finding the seats. They couldn't just order a bunch of folding chairs as if this was a PTA meeting. Even the prime minister of Andorra expected a cushion.

The betting was divided over what the message would be. Most thought it was going to be some friendly gesture, like curing cancer or making all our nuclear weapons disappear, while an increasingly paranoid minority insisted on vigilance against darker motives. Suddenly, everyone seemed to be referring to a decades-old episode of *The Twilight Zone* where benevolent visitors from another world arrive and announce their plans for turning Earth into Utopia are spelled out in a book called *To Serve Man*, which finally turns out to be a cookbook.

This hysteria was exacerbated when a "bimmie"—the lower echelon and often marginally employed support staff of the Catskills hotels—was reported missing. It turns out that the guy, an assistant baker, had lifted a case of vanilla extract out of the hotel pantry and gone off on his own days of wine and roses. When he was discovered in the back of the hotel laundry room, he hadn't even heard about the landing. In response to repeated questions shouted at the hungover worker about what the "aliens" had done to him, he fumbled open his wallet and pulled out his green card.

It was in this atmosphere that Ambassador Zetz Gezunt of the planet Brogard appeared before the General Assembly. He was alone. He had announced that he wanted to establish friendly relations with Earth and the principles for scientific and cultural exchange before allowing other Brogardi to appear. Though as uninvited as he was unexpected, the Ambassador was trying hard not to wear out his welcome.

The media coverage, as might be expected, blanketed the airwaves. Even MTV was pre-empted. After all, space aliens were guaranteed to be weirder than even the latest release from Lady Gaga in a meat dress. Who or what could possibly top this?

One thing hadn't changed, however. The politicians still had to put their two cents (or two centavos or two pesos or two rupees or two shekels) in before Ambassador Gezunt would be allowed to speak. So, for the next three and a half hours, he sat next to the Secretary-General as one world leader after another got up to welcome him. Each of the 192 members of the august body offered what each assumed was their own unique greeting but which quickly developed into a numbing sameness. The Ambassador's reaction to this explosion of hot air was totally unreadable. At least the television commentators assumed it was unreadable. He could have been laughing his ass off so far as we knew of Brogardi body language. Finally, the president of Zimbabwe wrapped up his greetings in English, chiShona and Sindebele, inviting the Ambassador to visit his country's scenic chromium mines, sheep ranches, and tea plantations. One might assume that Earth had decided on a strategy should the Brogardi turn out to be hostile: we were going to bore them to death.

Now, as the last of the member's speeches faded away, the world held its collective breath as the Secretary-General rose. Instead of begging the Ambassador for forgiveness, he redundantly proceeded to give *his* greetings, this time on behalf of the entire world. One would have thought that the 192 speeches already given had conveyed that message, but the Secretary-General wanted to make sure that no nuance—and no stomach—was left unturned. These remarks then segued into his introduction of the Ambassador, as if the Brogardi was the featured after-dinner speaker, and it was the Secretary-General's job to warm up the crowd. At this point, I think most of the viewing audience was ready to surrender to the alien invaders provided we never had to hear another political speech again.

It was now late afternoon, and Ambassador Gezunt finally arose to speak. As he had on the golf course only two days ago, what was striking about him was, first, that he looked very similar to us and, second, that he was blue. Once you got beyond that, other little differences stood out. The most obvious one was that he was hairless or, at least, bald. We didn't have any other Brogardi for comparison purposes yet. But while it turned out there was some color variation, the hairlessness was indeed a species trait. It appeared that Earth's barbers would not be benefitting from whatever trade was established between the two worlds. He also had two flapping pieces of tissue on either side of his throat that turned out to be some sort of vestigial gill. The Brogardi, we would discover, could easily stay under water for several minutes at a time, but couldn't actually survive down there.

He strode to the podium, looking decidedly human, and set down what looked like his notes. Before beginning, he took the glass of water there and had a sip. News anchors in dozens of languages speculated whether it actually was water, what his consumption of it might mean, and whether the Brogardi were here to replenish their own supply of the liquid by stealing ours. When he let out what sounded like a satisfied sigh, a consensus was reached: he had been thirsty.

Now refreshed, he was ready to begin. "Greetings, ladies and gentlemen of Earth," the Ambassador proclaimed. "This is the start of an exciting new chapter of history for both our peoples. While our differences are striking, so are our similarities. One major difference is that our planet, though made up of various populations, is under a single government. A major advantage of that is that when the first Earth delegation arrives on Brogard, you will only have to hear *one* welcoming speech."

This was greeted with wildly enthusiastic applause, each delegation assuming that *their* presentation was the only one that had been really necessary. When the ovation died down, he repeated his message in flawless French, Russian, Arabic, Spanish, and Chinese. The assembled delegates and leaders responded with renewed applause, as well as some intense murmuring. How had he done that? How had he *known* that?

"Since I am instructed that you have translation devices at your seats, I shall continue my remarks in English, but rest assured that we have people who are fluent in all Earth languages."

More murmuring. The Ambassador apparently had planned to move onto something else, but even a novice at human relations couldn't help but notice the very unsatisfied atmosphere in the General Assembly Hall. There was a pregnant pause, as he seemed to be making up his mind as to whether to stick to the prepared remarks or address his audience's concern over his linguistic fluency. Suddenly the choice was made, and he resumed.

"You're probably wondering just how we learned your languages. We first became aware of your existence when your broadcast signals started reaching Brogard, about thirty of your years ago."

This was no surprise. It was well known that our radio and TV signals had been zipping through space for years, providing an unusual calling card for our species. Indeed, the press had had a field day digging up old science fiction stories and movies in which alien cultures arrived looking for Ralph Kramden or Jed Clampett, assuming they were major figures in Earth's ruling class.

"Our scientists quickly pinpointed your planet as the source of these signals, but they also realized that the information they contained were greatly out of date, as they had been traveling at just under the speed of light. It wouldn't do to build our assumptions on this information, and then discover that you no longer followed such things yourself."

Now he had everyone's attention. If the Brogardi hadn't used old radio and television signals, then what was their source of information?

"Utilizing our new dimensional drive, we put probes in orbit around your planet to collect and bring back your latest broadcasts. One of the mysteries we've been trying to figure out is whether you've been developing more languages over the years, or simply that additional groups have gained technical facility."

That was actually a rather astute observation, given the information the Brogardi had to work with, but before he could continue, there was an outburst from the audience. "Now hold on, Mr. Ambassador," erupted the American president, who was not pleased. "Are you saying you have some sort of..." She leaned over to one of her aides, who whispered in her ear. "...some sort of cloaking device, so that we couldn't detect your satellites?"

Well, this was it. Were the Brogardi a race so scientifically advanced that humanity was like an idiot child in comparison, who could only hope to be treated kindly? Or would this confrontation rip the friendly mask away, and reveal them to be carnivores with an appetite for human flesh from *The Twilight Zone*?

"Cloaking device?" asked the Ambassador. "You mean like on *Star Trek*?"

This got a huge laugh from all of the press and most of the delegates, since the long-running sci-fi phenomenon had permeated most of the Earth nations and, apparently, the Ambassador's home planet as well. Delegates from North Korea and Yemen could be seen scurrying around the hall, looking for someone to explain the joke to them so they could inform their leaders. It defused the tension, but the question was still hanging.

The American president, chagrined, held her ground. "Well, Mr. Ambassador? We've detected none of your space probes in Earth orbit."

Now it was Ambassador Gezunt's turn to react. He made a series of gasping noises that sounded a little like he was having an asthmatic attack. The Secretary-General rose to offer assistance, but was at a loss for what to do. The Ambassador waved him away.

"I'm sorry. This is just so funny. Please forgive me for enjoying our little joke."

Joke? The wheezing was the Brogardi version of laughter. He was laughing at us. Now it was really getting creepy. Were all our astronomers going to turn out to be Brogardi spies?

"We realized we couldn't put anything in Earth orbit without your noticing, but we also discovered that you had a lot of debris there that you seemed content to let float around until it was finally destroyed in your atmosphere. What we did was replace these abandoned items with our probes, setting them on the same courses. This allowed us to monitor your broadcasts without anyone being the wiser."

Ambassador Gezunt stood at the podium, looking for all the world like a schoolboy expecting praise for his extremely clever solution to the math problem on the board. He clearly did not anticipate the reaction he did get, which was pandemonium. Delegates rose from their seats shouting, while the American president and the Russian premier huddled in discussion as to how quickly they could get their own forces into space. What the Ambassador had thought was a delightful trick was being taken as tantamount to an act of war.

"Please, ladies and gentlemen, you misunderstand. We knew that the first contact between our peoples had to be carefully prepared for and planned. It was never our intent to hide any of this from you."

The Secretary-General rose, gently elbowed the Ambassador aside, and did what he should have done four hours earlier: he told everyone to shut up. "We will speed up this process of opening up a dialogue considerably if we let the Ambassador complete his remarks without further interruption." All right, he's a diplomat. Translated into plainer words, that came out as, "Yo, stifle!"

Ambassador Gezunt returned to the microphone realizing that things were going badly for him. If he wanted to avoid war between his planet and ours, now was the time to act. "So there will be no doubt that we intended no harm, my colleagues are—at this moment—dispatching to each of your governments all the plans for the satellites, as well as our dimensional drive technology. We are also making available records describing the languages and customs of the peoples of Brogard. Our goal is for us to meet as equal partners, pooling our knowledge and resources for the betterment of both planets."

The various delegates, who had been blowing hot and cold all afternoon, rustled with interest. It sounded promising, but it hardly resolved things. It was obvious to everyone that he had the upper hand, and it was the Earth leaders who were at a disadvantage. The Brogardi were granting explanations and information, even the secret of supposedly impossible—under our science—faster-than-light travel. What could we possibly offer these superbeings in exchange for this bounty? Leave it to the Russians to get to the point.

"Mr. Ambassador, we thank you for your openness and honesty," said the Russian premier. "What can we possibly offer in return?"

In a day of surprises and lightning quick reverses, no one was expecting what came next. One could sense the whole world growing silent as we were told what price we would have to pay for the boon we had been offered.

"We have, indeed, learned a lot about Earth from our study of your ancient and modern broadcasts," he began. "Your languages, your customs, your histories, your philosophies… all this and more you have given us. Through it all, there was one thing that stood out, one area where the people of Brogard hoped against hope that you had indeed unlocked a mystery that you might share with our people."

Around the globe and across the hall, every human being within earshot of this speech leaned forward to catch the next words.

With noticeable hesitation, almost as if he feared what the answer would be, the Ambassador asked, "Is it true, is it really possible, that you have discovered the secret of anesthesia?"

Chaos broke out anew in the hall. Only this time the resulting tumult was filled with joy and celebration. Humanity and the Brogardi were going to get along just fine.

Starman

Ambassador Gezunt's tour de force at the United Nations had ensured that the Brogardi would be thought of as equals, not as some master race from the stars. They provided us with the secret of their dimensional drive, and after accounting for some differences in the Brogardi circulatory system—which explained why they were blue—we were able to modernize their medical practices from a level fixed somewhere, I'm told, around the area of our early 19th century.

I make no pretense to understanding the workings of the dimensional drive. Norm tried to explain it to me one afternoon, and after about twenty minutes my brain started to hurt. It has something to do with moving *between* the atoms that make up everything in the universe, but if you want the details, go look it up in *Scientific American*. I'm a studio tubthumper, not an astrophysicist.

What was amazing was just how quickly the Brogardi went from being the miracle of the millennium to being consigned to yesterday's news. Oh, we still liked them all right, and all the papers and news shows carried reports about them and about the first Earth delegation sent to Brogard, but we humans really do have short attention spans. The Brogardi were no longer a novelty. And that's good for me, because after the summer movie season from hell, Graham Studios had to make up for lost time. *The Ducklings' Space Adventure* had gone right to video because with blue men from outer space walking down our city streets, who wanted to see science fiction?

A few thousand Brogardi were now wandering around the Earth, sincerely trying to take the 192 invitations of hospitality they had been offered at the UN. A few of the national leaders were startled that their rhetoric had been taken at face value, but an interesting offshoot of the Ambassador's speech was that Earth's own conflicts had started to seem rather petty. Ronald Reagan had gotten it exactly wrong: it wasn't an enemy from the stars that was ending war on Earth, it was a friendly neighbor. Some pretty intractable problems had vanished almost overnight. After all, how did it look for the family to fight in front of company?

On this particular day in late November, I arrived in my office with nearly a dozen projects to deal with, several requiring immediate attention. Betty, as always, was fielding calls and messages in the outer office. A prim 70, Betty had been with the Graham Studios for years. In a business where 30 was considered old and 50 ancient, she had survived for a simple reason: she had made herself indispensable. Whenever anyone suggested retirement, she brushed it off with a "Don't be silly." Over the years, she had mastered electric typewriters and then computers, she could surf the Internet, she had programmed our office phone system, and she was able to locate any file I needed almost instantly. Her children were long grown, with families of their own, and her work in the movie business made her seem exotic to her grandkids. With company profit-sharing, she was self-sufficient, which made her a powerful figure in Hollywood: someone who didn't act out of fear of losing her job. I could have forced her out, I suppose, but I never could have lived with myself if I did. Hell, I hoped that I'd be as indispensable when I was her age.

"Good morning, Mr. Berman."

"Betty, how many times do I have to tell you: my *father* is Mr. Berman. You're older than he is. Please, call me Jake."

"Don't be silly, Mr. Berman," she said with a smile. This was a conversation that had turned into ritual. If I had one goal before one or the other of us finally stepped down, it was to have her call me by my first name. "Now, you've got the home video department wanting to discuss the Duckling holiday campaign, Ms. Carlyle wants to meet with you about the TV bookings for promoting our December releases, and Mr. Peterson is calling from the set of *Two on the Aisle*."

I accepted the stack of pink slips she handed me. The day had now officially begun. "Get me Fred Peterson on the phone please, Betty," I said as I headed into my office.

I liked my office. Rather than decorate it with movie posters promoting our greatest hits, I had but one bit of memorabilia on the wall: a framed poster of *Abbott and Costello Meet Frankenstein*. A wonderfully funny and scary movie, with a negative reputation among people who never seen it, I put it up just to keep everyone guessing. Was it ironic, or did I really mean it?

"Mr. Peterson on line 3," came Betty's voice through the intercom.

"Thanks." I picked up the phone to hear the frantic voice of our unit publicist on what we expected would be our comedy offering for next summer. *Two on the Aisle* was about two movie critics who co-host a TV show who can't stand one another in real life. We hoped it would be a winner.

"Fred? Jake. What's up?"

"It's them. They're really here."

"Calm down, Fred. *Who's* here?"

"The real ones. The two guys who do that cable show and podcast. They're on the set, doing a feature on our movie."

"Yes, go on Fred. That sounds like *good* news. Remember? We *want* publicity for our movies."

"You don't understand. They want to be *in* the movie."

That was a new one for me. Everyone wants to be in the movies, of course, but these two 800-pound gorillas could make life messy if we turned them down. "Fred, is Harry on the set? Put him on."

Fred went to get Harry Deutschman, producer of the movie, while I skimmed through the rest of the messages. "Jake? Harry. What do you think we should do with the critics?"

"Don't hand me a straight line like that this early in the morning, Harry. Now what is it, exactly, that they want?"

"They watched some of the filming, and they're rather tickled by it. When they met their onscreen counterparts, it was downright eerie. I wanted to start hanging crucifixes and cloves of garlic."

"So what do they want?"

"A walk on. Dex thinks we can improvise a bit this afternoon when we're shooting the press screening scene. I just wanted to make sure that was okay with you guys upstairs before we put two of the biggest movie critics in America *in* one of our movies."

I mulled it over. If Frank Dexter, the director, didn't mind them shoving their way into his film, who was I to object? "Let them do it," I said. "It'll be good for business. It will ensure they either give us a rave or keep their mouths shut. It also means if they decide they're insulted by the finished film, they'll be too embarrassed to sue."

"Thanks, Jake. You can see why I didn't want to wing this one on my own."

"I live to serve, Harry. Hang in there. Eighteen months from now, it'll just be another discounted video on the 'previously viewed' table."

Next up was the Ducklings release, since that was one of the mainstays of Graham Studios' business. Sylvester Graham, Senior, had bought the rights to this obscure collection of children's stories about a duck family that had adventures: they went to the zoo, they went on a zeppelin, they got audited. The first film, coming out just after the Nixon resignation, caught the national mood just right. *The Duckling's Washington Adventure* was an upbeat and patriotic story that went on to gross $60 million, absolutely phenomenal for a kid's film. Graham parlayed his success into his own operation, having been shrewd enough to secure the sequel rights for himself.

When he founded his own company, he modeled the operation on the classic Hollywood studios. According to legend, he was one of the last of the generation who had walked with the moguls. I should know. I helped draft the press release that created that legend myself. Truth be told, if the old moguls said anything to Sylvester Graham, it was more on the order of: "Kid, is the mail here yet?"

Eventually, Graham became a producer and then, coasting on the success of the first Duckling films, established his own production company. Realizing he would never compete in the big leagues, since the major studios had all become huge international corporations, he went for a niche. He would make a few films a year geared for families and for adults who wanted simple, user friendly entertainment. His films never grossed $200,000,000, but on the other hand, he never dropped anything even approaching that amount for a star-heavy, effects-laden bomb. By controlling costs, Graham films did steady, dependable business, with an occasional breakout hit every year or two. The failures would eventually make their costs back on home video, foreign sales, video on demand, and syndication, and everybody was happy, including our parent corporation. Noticing that Graham Studios always made a profit, they left us alone, instead of trying to squeeze more money out.

When Graham finally retired, his son, Sylvester, Jr., took over. Sly, as he was called to his face, or Junior, as he was called everywhere else, was also an original, breaking the mold of the Hollywood prince. Basically, there were two scenarios for the second generation. First, he could come in, decide to remake everything in his own image, and drive the studio into bankruptcy. Or, he could decide his father was a god, that every offhand policy his father promulgated was holy writ and never to be altered, and drive the studio into bankruptcy. Instead, Junior decided to emulate his father by sticking to what was economical and safe, but he also knew enough to tack with the prevailing winds. He would take calculated chances he could afford to lose, and avoided gambling the bulk of the studio's fortunes on the latest fad. When movies about computers got everyone in town to put their biggest stars on screen tapping at keyboards, Junior took the teenage boy from the Duckling family and ordered up a solo effort called *Webbed Site*. It made $30 million opening weekend, and we were still shipping home video units to the stores five years later. Graham Senior saw it about six months before he passed on, and told Junior he never would have dared to do a solo Duckling movie. Junior had shown initiative, and it had paid off. Senior died knowing his enterprise was in good hands.

Unfortunately, the summer had been devastating for the industry, not just Graham Studios. Who wanted to go to the movies when the adventure of a lifetime was playing for free on every channel on TV, as well as streaming across the Internet? Our problem was that, because we didn't have any blockbusters, we didn't have the huge cash reserves to coast through a downturn like this. That's why, when Betty told me "Mr. Graham, Junior" was on the line, I suspected we were getting ready for the cinematic equivalent of the Hail Mary pass.

Junior may have put his own mark on the studio, but he just couldn't bring himself to redecorate his father's office. Except for the obligatory picture of his wife and kids on his desk, it was set up in exactly the same style as his father had left it: late mogul. It was a huge office, with an entire meeting area for a dozen people at the front as you walked in. Then there was the expanse of carpet and, off in the distance, was THE DESK. Where it had come from was an ongoing topic of conversation at the studio. Some said it had once belonged to a president or governor, others said it was a prop from a movie that Senior had had smuggled off a sound stage one night when he was still learning the business working for other people. I happened to know that he had had it constructed himself, intent on the sole purpose of overwhelming anyone who had to approach it. That was the way the old guys did it, and that was the way he was going to do it, too.

Junior had inherited the desk, but not his father's imposing ways. He was tall and lanky, and his receding gray hairline and light moustache made him seem more like a museum curator who had lost his tour group than a studio chieftain. Junior had shown he could run the business on his own. It was just his misfortune that he didn't look the part. If his life was a movie, he'd have halted production and ordered the role recast.

Junior and I had a strange relationship. Although we were the same age, both in our early 40s, he was seen as the kid, while I was the veteran who been with his father since I was fresh out of college. So, for diplomacy's sake, I always made sure to go out of my way to defer to him. It was his studio, after all, and he was my boss. In turn, he made sure I was in on all corporate decisions, and frequently consulted with me privately, apart from other members of his executive team. I was a trusted advisor, so long as I remembered I was an advisor, and not the power behind the throne.

Speaking of which, this morning Junior was seated at his throne, behind the massive block of carved wood, reinforced steel, and chiseled marble that was THE DESK. Seated with his back to me was his guest, presumably the reason I had been summoned. I didn't know what was up, but the blue hand on the armrest told me something unusual was up. As it would turn out, I had no idea.

"Jake, glad you could take the time. I want to meet Abi Gezunt. He's going to be the first Brogardi to star in an Earth movie and *we've* got him."

Rising from his seat was a blue man wearing a Duckling polo shirt and a pair of chinos. He had apparently decided to go native. Standing a few inches taller than me at six feet, he extended his hand.

"Sly has been telling me all about the movie business, Mr. Berman. He said what you don't know isn't worth knowing."

"Pleased to meet you," I responded, to both his greeting and his hand-shake. I was trying to remember what title, if any, the Brogardi used for mister. "Abi Gezunt," I said, finessing my dilemma, "Any relation to…"

"He's my father," he replied.

"Abi has just been telling me that it's been his fondest wish to act," said Junior. "After making a careful study of the movie industry, he decided that Graham Studios was where he wanted to work."

"Your, um, stories are extremely tasteful," he said.

"Yes, I suppose they are… But I'm a little confused. Don't you have official duties to attend to? Aren't you part of your father's diplomatic mission?"

The Brogardi paused, as if uncertain just how much personal data to reveal. "You might say I'm more of a tourist. I have no official capacity. In fact, my father doesn't even know I'm here."

Hmm. The plot thickens. "So, Sly, what is it I can do for you?"

Junior pulled a cigar from the humidor on his desk, offering one to both Abi and myself, and smiling as we both declined. Since Graham Studios was a smokefree workspace, Junior wasn't going to light up, even in his own office. But the cigar was part of the mogul image, and his toying with the unlit stogie was a nod to his dear departed dad. It also gave him a few moments of silence to gather his thoughts and reassert his command.

"Abi here is going to be the first Brogardi movie star. If we do this right, we'll make up for all the money we lost last summer. But the important thing for us right now is secrecy. If this gets out, every studio in town will be wanting a Brogardi of their own, and some cut-rate operation will beat us to the punch."

Abi had what appeared to be a pained expression on his face. This turned out to be their way of smiling. "Are you all right?" I asked.

"Oh yes," he said. "I so enjoy the colloquial terminology in English. It's quite a colorful language."

"Yes," agreed Junior, a bit annoyed that his rhythm had been interrupted, but too polite—or too eager to close the deal—to let on. "So what I want you to do, Jake, is keep this under wraps. No publicity, not a word, until we're ready to premiere the film. And since Abi here is new in town, I'd like you to take him under your wing, personally."

"But Sly, I've got the Duckling campaign, and the Jean-Claude van Damme musical…"

"Delegate it. You can keep in touch with everyone by phone, but that's all secondary. *The Brogardi* is now the most important project at Graham Studios, and I want you to give it your utmost attention."

"*The Brogardi*? Is that your title, Sly?"

"It's tentative," he said, dismissing any objection with an airy wave. "Abi, I leave you in good hands." And with that, Junior spun around on his swivel chair to the work area behind his desk, and started going through his mail.

Abi continued to grimace, but didn't move. I leaned over. "If you think our colloquialisms are fun, just wait until you learn our body language."

"Pardon?"

"The meeting is adjourned."

On the way back to the office, I tried to figure out how I was going to relate to this aspiring star from space. "What do I call you? I'm not really clear on Brogardi rules of etiquette…"

He made that grimace again, showing that he was happy. "Please, call me Abe. It makes me feel *so* Hollywood."

"All right, Abe, let's brainstorm and see if we can figure out what we're going to do with you." He looked puzzled. "I'm sorry, is 'brainstorm' too colloquial?"

"I'm not sure. How are you using it?"

"Well, I meant we'd sit around and throw out ideas, eventually coming to a consensus as to what we should do."

There was a long pause before Abe finally responded. "Ah yes, I see. Brainstorm. Very good. We have a similar word, but it refers to a mental disorder."

Hoo boy. This was not going to be easy.

Betty's reaction almost made the whole thing worthwhile. Here was a woman who had seen everything, including a six-year-old grandson arriving for a visit sporting a Mohawk haircut, and taken it all in stride. A visitor from space strolling in with her boss was too much… for about ten seconds.

"Mr. Berman, there were some calls…" She stopped dead and took a good look at Abe. Then she let out a stream of sounds unlike anything I had ever heard. This brought a series of wheezes from Abe, who then made a series of similar noises. It was beginning to sound like the testing lab at a tissue factory.

The both looked at me and laughed, or at least, Betty laughed and Abe wheezed. "Your marvelous secretary asked if I was actually a Brogardi, or an Earthan going to a masquerade," he said. Turning to her he added, "Your pronunciation was excellent. The American accent is so charming."

"Betty? When did you have time to learn a foreign language?"

"I've been taking an evening class two nights a week. I'm hoping to go to Brogard on my vacation next year."

This delighted Abe even more. "You must visit the Floating Gardens. It is one of the most delightful attractions on my world."

"Have they reopened? I had understood there was some major replanting after the recent drought."

I stood there transfixed. How did she know this stuff? Maybe the Brogardi had been planting spies on Earth, and she was one of them. Abe, forgetting he was a tourist himself, began to expound enthusiastically on the delights of Brogard.

"When I left two weeks ago, they were getting ready for the rededication. Can I recommend a few out-of-the-way spots that the guidebooks tend to overlook..."

"I'm sure you can, Abe," I interrupted, "but Betty has her hands full right now, don't you, Betty?" I didn't wait for her response. "You're going to be spending a lot of time here. The two of you will have plenty of time to schedule her itinerary."

Betty did not seem at all pleased at my spiriting away Abe like that, but her vacation plans could wait. Junior had just presented me with a major problem: how was I supposed to keep the biggest story in Hollywood a secret?

The Brother from Another Planet

I decided discretion was the better part of valor, and opted to get Abe off the lot as quickly as possible, until we could figure out what to do with him. Larissa didn't know it, but we were about to get a houseguest.

"Abe, I think you should have an opportunity to get a taste of the good life. That's why I want you to stay in my home until we can get you settled in somewhere. Is that all right with you?"

Abe was having a bit of trouble at the moment, as he had discovered the button that controlled the electric window in the car. He let it fall and rise a couple of times, and then turned to me. "You know, Jake, you ought to consider being *my* guest on Brogard. There's nothing like seeing the ways of another culture to get you to view your own with fresh eyes."

"You got all that from a window?"

"Hmm? Oh no, I was just observing the variation in design. My vehicle's windows are more pliable, so they just roll up into the roof."

"Really?" It was bad enough having this conversation, without having to decipher what he was talking about. My mind was elsewhere. I was trying to navigate through midday traffic, hoping that no one would recognize my car and who my passenger was. Junior would have my head if I blew our cover before the first day was out. The only thing I was seeing clearly was the sign indicating my upcoming exit. Abe took my silence to be an invitation to continue the conversation.

"I would be delighted to stay with you, Jake. That's most generous. And you must allow me to help with the chores. Our Earthologists know from studying your broadcasts just how important *that* can be. I don't want any special privileges."

He was losing me again. "Chores? We've got a housekeeper for that, Abe. You're a guest. Relax. You'll have plenty of stuff to do once the movie gets underway. Now, the first thing we have to do is figure out what you can eat."

See, this is where my ostrich-like existence in the movie industry worked against me. I'm sure the news had been full of accounts of what the Brogardi eat, but if a story didn't affect the fortunes of Graham

Studios, it blew right past me. I would've been willing to bet any amount, however, that Betty could have told me precisely what they ate, including Googling a few recipes off the 'net.

"That's one of the most delightful things about us finding each other, Jake."

"What is?"

"I mean, our peoples finding each other. We're apparently much more alike than we are different. I can pretty much eat what I'd like off any Earth menu, provided I remember to take my supplements. The only thing I really don't like is chicken."

"Really?"

"It tastes a little too much like—" and here he offered another one of those Brogardi words that sounded like a cat gargling, "—well, I'm sure you can understand."

"Of course," I said.

"The memories are just too painful."

Just when I thought we were suddenly on the same wavelength, he lost me again. I forged bravely ahead. "No chicken, it is." While we were stuck at a light, I used my cell to send a quick message home to Rosa our housekeeper, to expect a guest for dinner and not to serve chicken. Any further explanation would have to wait.

It was early afternoon. Rosa was off doing the shopping, the kids were at school, and Larissa was still at her office and not due home until six. That gave us several hours of uninterrupted time to discuss Abe's plans, where he would live, and how we would ensure that he'd stay under wraps until the movie was ready for release. Even assuming that production could be sped up, I didn't see a premiere until sometime next spring. That would mean a good four or five months before we could go public, and there would be an awful lot of people who would know and would have to be convinced to remain silent. That, fortunately, could be left to Junior. I'm sure only his most trusted people would be involved, just as I was given the hardest job—babysitting Abe.

I took him downstairs to the family room, since it was less likely that an unexpected visitor would be able to spot him from the street. Fortunately, this was California, so there was virtually no pedestrian traffic at all. I had a frozen deep dish pizza in the oven—that would also require some explaining that could be postponed—and decided to have a drink.

"Abe, how are the Brogardi with alcohol?"

"Just wonderful. You know, your gravity is just a tad stronger than ours, and a good rubdown at the end of the day works wonders, at least I've found it to be so."

This was going to be a *very* long afternoon. "You know, Abe, one of the things I've been most impressed with is your fluency in English." He basked in the glow of my praise. "But, you know, our language can be maddeningly imprecise at times. When I asked you about alcohol, I meant *drinking* alcohol, not rubbing alcohol."

"Are they different?"

"Well, different enough. I just don't know enough about your dietary needs, and I would hate to give you something that backfired."

"Like when I was at that Mexican restaurant?"

I took a good look at him. That sounded a lot like he was making a joke, but I couldn't be sure. Then he started wheezing. "Did I get that right, Jake? I was intending a scatological joke, which our scholars report is a key to bonding among Earth males."

Now I started laughing. "Abe, you're okay. You got that exactly right. Now, what are you allowed to drink?"

I was behind the bar, pouring myself some bourbon and ice, while Abe pulled a small green book from his pocket and sat down, intently thumbing through it. "I'll tell you in a moment," he said without looking up.

"What's that, some sort of guide book?"

"Indeed. It has recommendations and warnings about your Earth foods. You wouldn't happen to have any Napoleon brandy, would you?"

This must be some guide book. "Sorry, Abe, I'm fresh out, and we haven't gotten today's delivery yet."

"All right then, I'll have a beer."

"No specifications? The experts don't recommend a particular brand?"

He looked down at the listing, and read the Brogardi advice on beer. "Any one with bubbles will do just fine, thank you very much."

"One beer with bubbles, coming up."

With the social preliminaries out of the way, and lunch not quite ready, it was time to focus on the task at hand. There were a lot of ways I could go around this, from strictly business to welcoming him into the family of Graham employees, but none of the standard approaches seemed right. After all, how often do you find yourself having a drink with a man from outer space in the middle of the afternoon, while waiting for a pizza to come out of the oven? Since we were going to be spending a lot of time together in the coming months, I thought it best to find out something about him. After the initial hoopla had died down, I hadn't really paid a lot of attention to the story, so I really didn't know much about his people or his planet. I'd have to get Betty to bring in some of her schoolbooks to the office—provided that they were in English.

"So, Abe, tell me something about yourself. Did you always want to be an actor? Do they have movies on Brogard?"

Abe took a long sip of beer, right out of the bottle. "These are good bubbles."

"Glad you're enjoying them."

"We don't really have movies, but there are re-enactments of the great stories of our people. I believe some of our books are available in translation now. I could get you one, if you'd like."

"That would be nice, Abe. Perhaps they'll use one of your stories for the movie."

"Oh, I don't think so. Sly told me he wanted to do an Earth story, a story about the friendship between your people and mine."

"That sounds like Junior, all right: nice and safe."

"Oh no, no, no. Sly was very clear about that. I told him that it would make Brogardi history."

I couldn't help feeling, even then, that perhaps I wasn't the right person for the job. Abe couldn't be friendlier, but perhaps I just wasn't astute enough for this. I kept feeling that there was something I needed to know, but I didn't know what question to ask.

"Tell me about your childhood. What was it like growing up on Brogard? What did you father do before he became ambassador to Earth?"

Suddenly, even I could tell the turn of the conversation was making Abe uncomfortable. He put the bottle down on the coffee table, and covered his eyes with his hands. Was he crying?

"Abe, I'm sorry. Did I say something wrong?"

"No, it's all right. My father and I do not have the best of relationships. He was in charge of the Earth project, making sense of all those broadcasts of yours, while I was a student living away from home. It is a stage of life not unlike your adolescence." He had removed his hands from his eyes, but still had trouble looking at me. He seemed to be fixated on the bottle on the table in front of him.

"Look, I didn't mean to pry. If this is private…"

"I was part of a group challenging the traditional ways. That's what I find so refreshing about Earth: it provides alternative ways of seeing life that can be quite different than ours, yet are perfectly rational and stable."

There it was again. Why did I feel like I was seeing a foreign movie with subtitles done by someone not fluent in the language? "Well, I remember my own college days. Here, young adulthood is a time for a little rebellion. It gives you a chance to find out who you are."

Abe finally turned and looked at me. "Exactly. That's exactly what it is. I want to act to find out who I am."

At that moment, the timer went off on the oven, and this train of thought was off to the railyards. "I'd love to hear more about this, but it's time for lunch. You'll find your bubbles go especially well with pizza."

I was just cleaning up the dishes and checking with Rosa about dinner when I heard the front door open.

"I'm home, I'm home, I'm home!" Hurricane Susan had just arrived home from school, having put in a hard day at kindergarten. Before I had a chance to cut her off at the pass, I heard a scream from the family room. I ran downstairs to find a startled Abe seated on the couch, and a shrieking Susan clutching her face in surprise.

"It's all right, honey, it's just—"

"A Brogardi! Yay!" With that she ran across the room without even a hello to her Daddy—and jumped into Abe's lap. I wasn't sure if such behavior was considered normal among the Brogardi young, but Susan moved too quickly for either of us to have a chance to react.

"My name is Susan and I'm five years old," she said, with great seriousness. "Who are you?"

"Now, Susan, you know better than that."

Abe let loose with that wheezy laugh of his and cut me off. "No, no, that's all right. It's one of the reasons I'm here. I want to see what a real Earth family is like." And with that, he turned his total attention to Susan. "So, you're five years old? That must make you very, very old. How many grandchildren do you have?"

Susan looked at him with a combination of delight and annoyance. "I'm not a grandmother, silly, I'm a little girl."

"You don't look so little to me," he answered.

"Well, I'm very grown up for my age. That's what Mommy says. Would you like to see my dolls?"

I attempted to intercede again. "Now dear, Abe and I have a lot of work to do."

"Is your name Abe? That's a funny name for a spaceman. At school we have a guinea pig named Stu. Do you have any pets?" Her mind moved like a pinball machine, with each idea ricocheting into something else.

"I would love to see your dolls," said Abe, selecting an earlier item from her smorgasbord of conversational volleys. "Do you have one of your father?"

"No, but I have one that you can give a bottle to. Would you like to feed her?" With that, Susan jumped off his lap and scurried out of the room, pausing briefly at the doorway to encourage him to follow.

I started to tell him to stay put, but he was having none of it. "I know you have to check in with Betty. I'm sure Susan can find something for us to do while you're on the phone."

Now that he mentioned it, I did have to call in for messages, and if I had any concern about Susan being afraid of a stranger from space, that didn't seem to be an issue. I picked up the phone as Abe sauntered after my daughter.

Betty seemed to be holding the fort just fine. I had told her to farm out inquiries to the staff, and hold only the most important items for me. I suppose it said something about my indispensability that there were only two messages for me, one of them from Larissa saying she'd be able to pick up the baby from daycare. I had Betty transfer me over to Dick Lyman, our vice president of operations.

"Lyman," he muttered, coming on the line. A former Marine, he never said hello or goodbye on the phone, as he had decided it was a waste of time. So I got right to the point.

"Dick, it's Jake Berman. I need one of the bungalows cleaned up and refurbished for one of our stars."

"Yeah, Junior told me. Hush hush and all that. So he's going to be living on the lot?"

"We agreed that made the most sense. It would only be during the six weeks of production, and the fewer people seeing him entering or leaving the lot, the better."

"Can do. When do you need it?"

"A.S.A.P. He's my houseguest at the moment."

"Next week's Thanksgiving, and we close down Wednesday, noon. The best I can give you is a week from Monday."

"It'll have to do."

"Good enough." And with that, he hung up. It looked like we would be having company for the holiday. I hoped he didn't think turkey tasted like chicken. The way Rosa prepared it, I was hoping it would at least taste like turkey.

My phone calls done, I headed upstairs to rescue Abe from Susan. As I hit the upstairs hallway, I heard peals of childish laughter mixed with Brogardi wheezing.

"And you're sure this isn't your sister?" Abe was asking, holding a large, plush rabbit. They were sitting on the edge of her bed, surrounded by about a dozen of her dolls.

"No," shouted Susan, "That's Mr. Bunny. My sister is a baby."

"Ah, I see. I'm going to have spend a lot of time with you learning your language. You're very good at it. Have you been speaking it a long time?"

"All my life," she replied, without a hint of irony. Spotting me in the doorway, she ran over and gave me a big hug. "Daddy, Abe said he'd be my new best friend and come to my birthday party next month and teach me a song from his planet—"

"Whoa, hold on there, my little wildcat. We've got to set some rules here."

"Did I overstep my bounds?" said Abe. He sounded a little sad, and I think he looked that way, too. I was beginning to recognize his expressions.

"Well, remember we're trying to keep this a secret. If Radio Free Susie starts broadcasting, it's only a matter of time before somebody finds out."

"Does that mean he can't be my friend?" Now it was Susan's turn to pout.

"No, of course not. Abe will be staying with us for a little bit, and once he has his own place, he'll still visit quite often. But for the time being, you can't tell anybody."

"Why not?" she said, with a hint of a whine.

"Well, do you know what a secret is?"

"You mean like when you dropped Mommy's watch in the disposal, and you told her you didn't know how it got broken?"

I cleared my throat. "Yes, sort of like that. So for now, you can't tell anybody about Abe. It will be our secret."

A very disappointed Susan seemed to be on the verge of tears. It was then that I noticed that Abe seemed to be signaling me with some urgency.

"Yes, Abe?"

"Correct me if I'm wrong, Jake, but once the movie is released, then there's no cause for secrecy any more, is there?"

"No, of course not."

"And when do you expect that to be?"

"Sometime in the spring, no later than next May."

"Then by next May, Susan can tell everyone?"

I mulled that over. Diplomacy seemed to run in the Gezunt genes. "I don't see any reason why not."

Abe turned to Susan. "Is that okay with you? It's very important to your daddy and to Sly…"

"Sly? Who's that?"

"Sly Graham. Your dad and I are working for him."

"Oh, you mean Junior."

I shot her a look, but it was to no avail. I'd have to hope that it was lost on Abe.

"So can you keep a secret right now, and then later we'll tell everybody?"

"Everybody? You mean even Tommy Zucco who has *two* dogs?" That last was directed at me. With my allergies, we couldn't have any dogs, and Susan had taken my ailment personally.

"Everybody. Even Tommy Zucco *and* his two dogs." With that, she leapt off the bed and started dancing around. "Abe and me have a secret! Yay!"

"I hope your mother takes it this well," I said, to no one in particular.

The Food of the Gods

I really had to hand it to Larissa. She walked in the front door holding Elizabeth, the baby's food bag, the baby's clothing bag, and her own briefcase. She was greeted by me, a frenetic Susan, and Abe. She took us all in at a glance, decided all explanations could wait, and said, "Can someone take something please?"

I picked up Elizabeth so that Larissa could sort the bags for later emptying and refilling in the appropriate parts of the house. I decided that at least an introduction was in immediate order.

"Dear, I want you to meet Abi Gezunt. He's going to be staying with us for the next week."

All right, so I rounded it off a bit. Like, by a week. Larissa again instantly processed the information, and determined that any discussion as to why she was learning about this in this manner and at this time could wait. I knew it was merely being postponed, but I was grateful for the effort.

"Mr. Gezunt, it's a pleasure to meet you." She extended her hand, and then paused. "I'm sorry, do you shake hands?"

"Actually, no, but—to paraphrase one of your sayings—when on Earth, do as the Earthans do," he replied, grasping her hand. "Your custom has a history, so I'm told. I understand it was to demonstrate that you were unarmed and posed no danger to the other person."

"Really? I had no idea."

While Larissa was being gracious and Abe was being pedantic, the two Berman children had other ideas. Elizabeth was letting me know in no uncertain times that it was time for a diaper change, while Susan had had enough of adult conversation and wanted to go back to playing with her new best friend. There were at least half a dozen of her dolls to which he had yet to be introduced.

"Larissa? The baby needs changing."

Larissa looked at me. "Yes? So go take care of it. I just got home."

"Perhaps this would be a good time for Susan to finish giving me the tour of her room," suggested Abe. I nodded gratefully, then wondered if nodding was one of the things we had in common or not. It didn't matter; they were off to see Mr. Bunny's relations, including a stuffed moose doll that was almost as big as Susan. It had been a gift from Junior, and cost a small fortune. It had also been left over from last year's Showeast convention for the nation's theater owners. We had brought it along for display purposes, since the moose was the company logo. Rather than pay to have it stored, he gave it to Susan, saving himself the warehouse fee, and with the full knowledge that he could always borrow it back if he needed it.

That left Larissa and me alone with a baby that was now balancing her state of wetness at one end by crying hysterically on my shoulder, trying to get just as wet at the other end. I headed off to the baby's room and undressed her. If I was going to change her diaper this late in the day, I might as well put her in her pajamas. Larissa followed behind after dropping off the various bags around the house and checking on the state of dinner. Closing the door behind her, she waited until I had disposed of the soiled diaper before firing the opening salvo of our argument.

"He's staying with us for a week? Couldn't you have at least called and warned me, instead of springing it on me as I walk in the door? You know I hate surprises like that."

Diaper on, I proceeded fastening the several dozen—or so it seemed— snaps on her undershirt and pajamas. Whoever designs baby clothes is a sadist. Either that, or it's someone who has never actually met a baby. If it was up to me, it would all be Velcro or the zipper-like seals that they have on sandwich bags that you just squeeze shut. At least the concentration involved in lining up all the snaps and then snapping them shut—all the while baby Elizabeth was letting me know she was going to attempt to exercise her prerogative to be somewhere else—allowed me to ignore Larissa's questions for the moment.

The last snap done, I handed the baby over to her, figuring it might have a calming effect.

"You told me you were in the middle of a murder trial. I could have interrupted the proceedings, but I didn't think it would get you in good with the judge." Larissa is a court reporter, and is virtually impossible to reach when she's doing a trial. Of course I hadn't tried to reach her, but it was a good excuse and I was sticking with it.

"Who is he? Why is he here?"

I quickly sketched in the details of Abe's coming to work at the studio, and how we had to keep him under wraps. "They promise me that his bungalow on the lot will be ready as soon as they reopen the studio after Thanksgiving."

"That's nearly two weeks. Where is he going to stay? What are we going to feed him? What about the children?"

"Which question do you want me to answer first?"

"Try this one: do you think the jury will let me off if I kill you right now?"

"Look, this is probably the biggest movie I'll ever be involved with, if not the most historic one in the entire history of the industry. The most important job right now is keeping Abe happy and safe and in seclusion. That job was given to me. Don't forget that I did lots of things I didn't like when you were president of your state association, including going to those meetings where I was the only spouse there who wasn't another court reporter. So now it's your turn to be there for me."

"Like going to all those boring awards shows and charity events isn't being there for you."

"Yes, I know how burdensome it was to be all dressed up and having to spend the whole evening chitchatting with George Clooney or Brad Pitt."

"You'll remember I came home with you."

"It was their loss."

She put Elizabeth down in her baby swing and turned it on. Then she rose and gave me a hug. "Of course your space alien can stay here. And I'm sure we'll have a wonderful time. But what are we supposed to feed him?"

"Apparently, anything except chicken."

Dinner that evening was a smashing success. Elizabeth was already asleep, and the four of us enjoyed salad, melon, and a main course of sand dabs, a Pacific Ocean fish that Rosa prepares just right. The only problem occurred with the vegetable, which was broccoli.

"Mommy, I don't like broccoli," insisted Susan, with all the persuasive powers accorded to her at age five.

"Nobody likes broccoli," I muttered under my breath, "Just shut up and eat it."

"Now Susie, you know you have to at least try everything on your plate. Broccoli is good for you. And it's really quite tasty." To prove her point she speared a green floret and popped it in her mouth. "See? And Daddy eats his broccoli, too."

"Actually, I'm stuffed…" I began, until Larissa shot me a look that indicated I would eat some broccoli now, or be condemned to discussing my failure to do so for the rest of my life. "That's right, Susie. Everyone eats their broccoli." I picked up a small piece and tried to get it from mouth to stomach in the fewest possible moves. The glass of Pinot Grigio helped.

Susan watched this display with some satisfaction. If she was going to be tortured, then everyone had to suffer. Then she paused. "What about Abe?"

"Quite right, I must eat my broccoli, too." He bit down into a piece, and appeared to wince. A second bite brought a renewed look of pain. I was pretty sure that this grimace was the universal symbol for, "I hate broccoli."

"Oh, please, Abe, you're our guest. You don't have to eat your broccoli if you don't want to."

"How come Abe doesn't have to and I do?" Her tone suggested that the American Civil Liberties Union would be receiving a call in the morning, asking if the Fourteenth Amendment's "equal protection" clause applied to the Berman dining room.

"Because Abe is our guest and Abe is a grown up. But Mommy and Daddy are eating their broccoli." She took another bite and motioned me to do the same. At this stage, I was willing to concede the point to Susan. I agreed with her. I've never liked this vile substance, either. In fact, it was one of the few issues on which I had agreed with George H.W. Bush. Fortunately, Abe came to the rescue.

"According to my guidebook, broccoli is a good source of vitamin C, biotin, and riboflavin." He looked at Susan. "Are you getting enough riboflavin?"

"Riboflavor? What's that?"

Abe appeared startled, as if he wasn't expecting his guidebook to be questioned. "I don't know," he said, "but the book says we need to have it, and it's in broccoli. Why don't we each eat one to make sure we're getting enough?"

He took another bite of broccoli and grimaced. This made Susan laugh. "Now it's your turn," he told her.

She took a bite, and made exaggerated faces in return. This went back and forth, and by the time they were through, they had each eaten about half the vegetables on their plates.

"Perhaps we should have corn tomorrow night," suggested Larissa, clearly not eager for a repeat of this display.

"What's for dessert?" I asked Rosa, who had come in to clear the plates. "I think we really earned it tonight."

After dinner, Larissa went off to give Susan her bath and get her ready for bed. Abe and I sat on the back deck. It was a cool, California evening. Lit only by the lights in the house, we were virtually invisible to our neighbors.

"I'm sorry if my staying here caused any trouble," Abe said, but I cut him off before he could go on.

"Larissa was simply startled, that's all. Of course, next week—when her father is here for our Thanksgiving holiday dinner—might be a different story."

"Why is that?"

"Because her father is a bigot. He doesn't like foreigners, and he's not especially fond of even Americans who come from other parts of the country. I don't know what he'll make of you. He'll probably start complaining about the Martians."

"Well, we're in luck then," said Abe. "Brogard is in a different stellar system entirely."

I wasn't sure if that was a joke or not. "Do you have prejudice where you come from?"

"How do you mean?"

"Well, for example, Larissa's father hates everybody from New York. He grew up in New York City, and thinks it's a dirty, money-grubbing place, and he was glad to come out here to retire. He once met someone at a party from the city of Rochester, which is upstate, several hundred miles away from New York City, and took an immediate dislike to him.

The funny thing is, according my mother-in-law, it turned out the guy from Rochester hates New York City, too."

Abe appeared somewhat baffled. "I'm not quite sure I follow. You mean Larissa's father dislikes someone based on where he's from, not who he is individually?"

"Where's he from, what his religion is, what groups he belongs to, what color his skin is… I don't believe he's expressed any opinion on blue skin, but I'm sure we'll find out."

"You'll pardon me for saying this, Jake, but the man sounds somewhat irrational."

"No 'somewhat' about it. He's completely prejudiced. The National Conference of Christians and Jews wanted to give him an award for being such a perfect bad example for everyone else. You have anything like that on Brogard?"

"Not at all. I find it a very alien concept."

I sighed. Here was something Brogard had to teach Earth. This might be the basis for our movie. I'd have to remember to tell Junior about this in the morning. "I know this doesn't put Earth in the best light, Abe, but you make Brogard sound like a utopia, without any hatred or fighting."

Abe sat up with a start. "Who said we had no hatred or fighting? Oh my, we have enough of that for dozens of story cycles in just a single season. Sometimes the violence gets completely out of control."

Now it was my turn to be baffled. "But you said…"

"…that we have no prejudice. Anyone who hates another person has a reason specific to that person. It would be foolish for me to dislike a Bro-gardi because his skin was a lighter or darker blue than mine, or because he grew up on the Southern Continent and I grew up on the Western."

"So why would you fight?"

"Well, take my mother's brother's son, Kuni Lemmel. When I was, oh, it would be roughly ten years old in your terms, I had not gone to school one day. I was a good student and enjoyed my studies, but I wanted to experience what it would be like to break the rules, to not do what was expected of me."

"You played hooky."

"No, I walked along the river… Oh, I see, that was one of your colloquialisms again." He pulled out his little guide book and scribbled a note to himself, holding it up to the light coming from the kitchen window. "In any case, Kuni saw that I wasn't in school, and told his father, who told my mother. Naturally, she told my father, and he punished me rather severely."

"Was this a major infraction?"

"On Brogardi, no. It wasn't encouraged, of course, but it was understood that developing children need to test limits by a little harmless rulebreaking now and then."

"So what was the problem?"

"Well, my father was not a typical Brogardi. His son was not going to be an ordinary child. You saw me trying to eat your broccoli tonight? My punishment was many times worse, and it lasted for an entire season."

"Wasn't that rather severe?"

Abe made what I had come to understand was his "unpleasant experience" face. "Yes, it was. And if I saw Kuni in front of me right now, I'd have to give him a thorough thrashing."

"Let me understand this, Abe. This cousin of yours ratted you out when you were a kid, and you're still holding a grudge? Didn't you get even with him then?"

Abe paused as if he was digesting what I had said. Then he gave his laughing wheeze. "Ratted you out. That's a very good one. I'll have to remember that. Yes, of course I took my revenge then, but the score is far from settled. This may go on for a long time to come."

I thought about that. "I'm sure glad you have no prejudice on Brogard, Abe. I don't think your people would be able to handle it."

Susan was all tucked in, and it was time for her bedtime story. I always hated to miss this time of day, because it was a special father-daughter moment. We had started with baby board books—some of which had survived for Elizabeth to inherit—and she was now beginning to enjoy the collected works of Dr. Seuss on her own. My job, besides helping her drift off to sleep, was to read a chapter from a more advanced children's classic. Currently, we were working our way through *Winnie the Pooh* and *The House at Pooh Corner* for the second time, and we had just finished our favorite story, when they fail to find the mysterious "heffalump."

Larissa had gotten her into bed, and I brought Abe along to say goodnight. I started to pull *Pooh* off the shelf, when Susan said, "Can't Abe tell me a story tonight?"

"I don't think I had better," he said quickly. "Besides, I want to see the way you do things on Earth, not bring my Brogardi ways with me. Perhaps some other time, Susan."

Susan accepted that her friend didn't want to tell her a story, and let it go at that. She sat up so that Larissa could lean over for a good night kiss, and then motioned Abe over so he could receive his. He was apparently aware of the Earth habit of social kissing in various contexts, but his awkwardness made it clear that it was not one with which he had grown up.

Larissa indicated to Abe they should leave, as I sat on the edge of the bed to begin our ritual. Susan turned the pages of the book to the story she wanted to hear tonight, and handed it to me. I picked it up and began to read about Kanga and Baby Roo in the Forest.

While I read Susan the story, Larissa made up the guest room for Abe. Fortunately, it had a separate bathroom, so he could have complete privacy. Again, our ignorance on just how similar—or dissimilar—the Brogardi were from humans had us at a disadvantage. He told us he slept about seven hours a night which, given the hours we kept with baby Elizabeth, meant at least one of us would probably be up when he was.

"I opened up the couch and brought in the bedding, but he put all the pillows under his feet. He said he sleeps better with his feet raised," Larissa said.

"If he's happy, then Junior is happy, and I'm happy."

We were in the kitchen, figuring out with Rosa what leftovers to freeze and which to dispose of when Abe came in. He was still fully dressed.

"You know, Abe, it occurs to me that you don't have any luggage. Where are your belongings?"

"Back at the embassy in New York. I'd just as soon leave my stuff there if you don't mind. I'm rather enjoying my Earth clothes."

Larissa looked at his Ducklings shirt. "Well, you're going to need more than what Jake can pick up at the company store," she said, turning to me. "Dear, I'm sure you can arrange to get our guest everything he needs."

Everyone seems to be certain what responsibilities I'm able to take on. No matter. We were just biding time until Abe's studio home was ready and the film was set for production. "I'll figure something out in the morning."

"That's wonderful," said Abe, "Now, can I trouble you for some baking soda?"

Baking soda? What strange Brogardi ritual required that at this hour? We had absolutely no idea as to what ablutions the Brogardi performed, or how they performed them.

"No problem," I said, pulling the box off the shelf. "Is this a substitute for some kind of Brogardi item you need?"

"Actually, my guidebook said a little baking soda dissolved in water is good for indigestion. I'm afraid my system is still struggling with the broccoli."

I handed him the box while Larissa gave him a glass of water and a spoon. I made a mental note: No chicken. No broccoli.

The next morning was festive, as Rosa presented us waffles for breakfast and Susan introduced Abe to the joys of maple syrup. Larissa made do with an English muffin and coffee. She had had to take in a lot of fluids during the few months that she was breast feeding Elizabeth, and these days seemed too tired to have breakfast.

"But Mrs. Berman, breakfast is the most important meal of the day," insisted Rosa.

"I know," Larissa replied, sticking the bottle of formula in Elizabeth's mouth. "That's why I'm feeding the baby."

Abe had no trouble succumbing to Rosa's entreaties for seconds, and insisted she show him how they were made. While he was off in the kitchen getting a lecture on the varied uses of the waffle iron, the phone rang. It was Junior.

"Good morning, Jake. How's our little movie star?"

"Learning how to make waffles in Spanish, I think. Isn't it a little early for you to be in the office?"

"It's almost lunchtime in New York," he said, not pausing for any discussion of this non sequitur. "Dick tells me he's going to have the bungalow ready after the holiday. I told him not to spare any expense. You might bring Abe by to get his specifications."

"Will do, chief."

"Next, the script. Since time is of the essence on this, I've got somebody working on the scenario right now. We should have a script by mid-December, and be in pre-production by New Year's. Start thinking about the advertising campaign. We've got to get a teaser trailer out with our holiday product that gets everyone excited about our film without telling them anything."

"Not telling people anything is my specialty."

"Good," said Junior. He was so gung ho on this project that I couldn't even get a rise out of him with sarcasm. It was something he let me get away with in private conversations, but he usually took it as a challenge to one up me. Not this morning. "How's the family? They're treating Abe okay?"

Clearly the second question was the important one. "Everyone's doing just fine, Sly. Abe is already learning what it's like to be a star."

"Well, don't wear him out. Keep up the good work, Jake. Speak to you later."

Soon it was rush hour, as Susan boarded the school bus, and Larissa headed out to the courthouse, taking Elizabeth to day care on the way. Ordinarily, I'd be joining this frenzy as well, but this morning my job was sitting at the other end of the table, soaking up the last of his maple syrup with a final bit of waffle.

"This stuff is wonderful. This is going to be a taste sensation on Brogard."

"Glad you enjoy it."

"Do you know how they do it?" he asked.

"Do what? Make waffles?"

"No, turn those huge maple trees into syrup."

It was going to be a long day.

Naturally, I couldn't just go strolling with Abe down Rodeo Drive. A Brogardi might attract attention, but would no longer be considered extraordinary. And, in California, where the unusual quickly becomes the mundane, people might ignore Abe in favor of this week's hot new rock star. However, a Brogardi being shepherded by the head of publicity at Graham Studios was another story. Within an hour of our appearance, it would have been circulating at *Daily Variety*, *The Hollywood Reporter*, *Entertainment Tonight*, and every hairdresser in town. By day's end, there wouldn't be a studio executive who didn't know that Graham had greenlighted a Brogardi project. No, this was going to take a subtler mind, someone able to handle extremely confidential work without attracting the slightest bit of attention.

"Good morning, Mr. Berman, Abe."

I looked at Betty in exasperation. "How come he's Abe and I'm Mr. Berman?"

"Don't be silly," she said, handing me a stack of phone messages, and picking up her steno pad. "I understand there's some shopping to do."

The three of us headed into my office, after Betty notified the switchboard that I wasn't taking any calls, and to route everything to voicemail. I went to my desk to sort through my messages, while Betty surveyed Abe, who was dressed in the same chinos and Ducklings polo shirt he'd worn yesterday.

"Let's start with the clothes. We can take measurements after. I'd say a dozen shirts, half a dozen slacks, a couple of sports jackets, socks and underwear... um, you do wear undergarments, don't you?"

Abe looked Betty squarely in the eye, "Well, perhaps we do, but my instructions are to vaporize myself before revealing that secret to you Earthans."

She stared at him in shock, until he started wheezing. "You're incorrigible," she said, like a mother scolding a favorite child.

"I'm trying to practice my acting," he said. For all I knew, he meant it. "Yes, of course we wear undergarments. But I'll tell you this: I refuse to wear a brassiere."

Betty looked steadfastly at her pad. "I think we'll be able to accommodate you. As for leisure clothes, I think we can throw in some items from the Graham Studio Store, at least around the house. I suppose we should get you some formal clothes, too, as well as some shoes. I'll take you down to wardrobe to get measured when we're through here."

There were half a dozen messages, with most of them being from Junior. There was also a note from Dick Lyman telling me not to call back, but that he was speeding up the rehab of the bungalow, and Abe would be able to move in the Friday afternoon after Thanksgiving. Apparently, Dick had been getting calls from Junior as well. That would work out well, since it meant Abe would have the weekend to settle in without any demands on his time.

"Now, what about toiletries?" Betty was asking.

"Jake's house has several. There's even one next to my room."

"No, no. Not toilets. Toiletries. What do you use by way of soap, toothpaste, shampoo… oh."

Abe patted his blue scalp. "I'm afraid I wouldn't have much use for shampoo. Don't need toothpaste either. Without any anesthesia, we developed a permanent coating for our teeth that's put on in childhood. My teeth will outlast me by several centuries."

"Betty, see if you can find out what's best for Brogardi indigestion. If Abe here gets into another broccoli eating contest with my daughter, he's going to need whatever advantage Earth science can give him."

Betty continued scribbling on her pad. "Is there anything else we can get you?" she asked.

Abe thought for a moment. "Well, I don't think I'll need this until I move into my own unit here at the studio, but can you get me one of those machines for watching your movies…"

"I think he means a DVD player," I suggested.

"Yes, that's right. I'll have some time on my hands once I move in, and I thought, if I'm going to be a movie actor, I ought to watch some Earth movies. Maybe I can pick up a few pointers."

"This is Hollywood, Abe. Watching movies is everybody's job. Getting you a DVD player won't be a problem. Betty, get him a large screen TV as well. Check with Dick Lyman's people and see if the bungalow has room for a projection screen. If not, get him the biggest set you can."

"I'm on it, Mr. Berman. Come on, Abe, you can tell me about Brogardi vacation spots while we get you measured."

"Call me Jake," I said, but I was already alone.

Mars Attacks!

The arrival of Larissa's parents for Thanksgiving was always a special treat. Never for a moment would I deny my girls the special pleasures of interacting with their grandparents, but with Abe in the house, the day was filled with potential disasters. The first one I headed off myself. I concocted a story about how Abe's visit to Hollywood was part of a goodwill tour, and that Junior would be visiting Brogard sometime in the future.

"So you run a studio on Brogard?" Larissa's mother asked innocently, when Abe came to join us. Claire was a retired elementary school teacher, and years of dealing with first graders had put a crimp in her conversational style. If she had a second glass of wine, her voice would slip into the sing-song cadences she used on generations of six-year-olds. I was debating whether to cut her off, or pour her the second glass myself.

"No, Mrs. Nathan, I came after my father was named permanent ambassador to Earth. I had just completed my education on Brogard."

"You see, Sidney," she said, slapping her husband on the knee, "I thought he had the same name as the ambassador."

Sid looked at Abe and smiled wanly. Like most people with prejudices, he was cowed into silence when actually in the presence of the object of his scorn. Actually, I think he was afraid that Abe was going to pull some sort of Martian ray gun on him. He got up and helped himself to another glass of wine. If I played this right, he could pass out this afternoon on the lounger, and we wouldn't have to wake him up until dinner.

"Grandpa! Come see my moose!"

Susan's call immediately transformed him from dozing graybeard to dynamic patriarch. He got to his feet with a big smile. "Do I hear one of my favorite granddaughters calling me?"

Susan stopped dead in her tracks. "I thought I *was* your favorite."

He picked her up and whispered just loud enough for the rest of us to hear. "Of course you are. But I didn't want Elizabeth to think I didn't love her too."

He was obviously banking on either Susie's forgetfulness, or his own mortality, before Elizabeth was old enough to object to this blatant favoritism. They wandered off together to see Junior's moose.

Meanwhile, Claire had sat down next to Abe on the couch. "Being an alien must be so fascinating. Tell me all about it."

"It's not that difficult, really. I wake up on Earth and there I am: an alien. But I'll let you in on a little secret." He leaned over to share his confidence conspiratorially. "If you and your husband were to be guests in my family's house back home, you'd be the space aliens. People would come from all over the continent to see you, and we'd have to make sure the little children weren't frightened by your, ahem, hair." He gestured at her delicately arranged, blue rinse special.

Claire looked at him in alarm. She couldn't tell if she was being insulted, or if he was pulling her leg. I suspected he was doing a bit of both. I was coming to really enjoy having Abe around. Meanwhile, my mother-in-law decided this was a joke, and she should be a good sport. She laughed, patting Abe's leg. "You almost had me there for a moment."

"And if you were a guest in my family's home, I certainly would have you, unless you brought your own spaceship with you," Abe said, with his characteristic wheeze. He then leaned over and gave Claire a good pat back on her own leg. Hmm, maybe Brogardi metabolism wasn't exactly human after all. Perhaps I ought to make sure he started slowing down a bit.

Sid came back with Susan after a few minutes. It was one thing to play the doting grandfather for a short while, but he found actually being one quickly grew tiring. He fell back into the lounge chair, while Susie fussed over her sister, who was enjoying a bottle on the couch next to Larissa. Sid might try to play favorites, but Susie remained protective of her sister. Sibling rivalry wouldn't kick in for a number of years yet.

"So, how are you enjoying retirement, Sid?" I asked.

I wasn't required to have actual conversations with him very often, but I thought when we were under the same roof, I should at least make the effort.

"As well as can be expected. The golf is great, but there are just too many damn New Yorkers who move out here."

"Dad," interjected Larissa, "you're a New Yorker who moved out here."

"That's different. After all, I always hated New York. But these people come out here and they try to turn Los Angeles into another one of the outer boroughs. Who needs Staten Island on the Pacific Ocean?"

"That's a good point, Mr. Nathan. I've noticed that, too. There are entirely too many New Yorkers here. Why don't they all go back where they came from?"

Sid looked over at his unexpected ally. In fact, we all kind of looked at Abe. Was he serious? Did he even realize what he was saying? Sid decided not let it go by, "What do you have against New Yorkers, Mr. Gezunt? Don't all humans look alike to you?"

"You know what the problem with New York is? It's entirely too close to Rochester."

"What's Rochester got to do with it?"

"And the people from Syracuse are even worse," Abe said, leaning toward Sid. "All of them."

"Oh, Rosa," called Larissa, walking toward the kitchen, "maybe it's time to serve the hors d'oeuvres."

Abe calmed down (read: sobered up) by the time we sat down to the family dinner an hour later. Susie had diplomatically invited him to talk to Mr. Bunny before her grandfather could start asking him where he came by his strong views about upstate New York. It was obvious that Sid was not only baffled by Abe's remarks, but he didn't see himself reflected in them at all.

While the food was being brought in, I was strapping Elizabeth into her high chair. She'd already been fed, but she could have her bottle and enjoy seeing the family. Personally, I was wondering if perhaps I should be strapped in as well, given the way the day was going.

Susan was seated between Abe and her grandmother, trying not to make it too obvious who she'd rather be talking to during dinner. Larissa was in the kitchen, supervising the display of the turkey. By family tradition, it was brought out for everyone to ooh and aah at, and then returned to the kitchen, where the carving and hacking could take place in privacy.

"Susie, are you going to monopolize your new friend all evening?" Subtlety was not Claire's long suit. As it turned out, her granddaughter had inherited this trait.

"Shh! It's a secret," Susan fairly shouted.

"What's a secret, dear? And you don't have to yell. I'm seated right next to you."

"Abe being my friend is a secret. We're not supposed to tell anybody because…"

"… because it wouldn't be fair to the children to subject them to all that media attention, wouldn't you agree, Mrs. Nathan?" Abe was smooth all right. He may not have much experience in Hollywood, but he clearly understood playing to a competitive advantage over your rivals. It wouldn't do to have to depend on Sid and Claire to enter into Junior's conspiracy.

"I quite agree, Mr. Gezunt."

"Please, Mrs. Nathan. Call me Abe."

Sid, feeling neglected, shouted in the direction of the kitchen, "Are you still trying to catch that turkey?"

"Perhaps Susie would like to explain to our guest what Thanksgiving is all about," encouraged Claire. "Would you like to have Susie tell you… Abe?"

"I'm always interested in whatever Susan has to tell me. We've become great friends…," Abe replied. Susie looked up at him in alarm. "Ah yes. Shh! It's a secret." He gave her a wink.

Susie struggled to remember just what they had said in class about this great American holiday, and then order it in her own mind so she could make her presentation. "Okay. The pilgrims came here and had a turkey with the Indians, and so now we all have a turkey with cranberry sauce and say thank you."

Before she had the chance to elaborate, Larissa came in to herald the arrival of the turkey. Rosa carried it around the table so that everyone could take a look, with Abe being especially fascinated by the stuffing which had been partially scooped out. Rosa departed to do the carving—a job for which she was far more qualified than I, and for which she received a hefty holiday bonus—while we undertook what little in the way of ritual our family had for Thanksgiving.

"I think this family has a lot to be grateful for this year," I began. "We're all in good health, and we welcomed Elizabeth into the fold with great excitement and great love." Elizabeth hit her bottle with her free hand, possibly as a sign of acknowledgment.

"While my parents won't be able to come from Florida until next month, they are doing well, and Larissa's parents—Sid and Claire—are here to enjoy their grandchildren. Susan has started school where, I understand, she is excelling at finger-painting and being able to read the entire alphabet…"

Susie beamed in appreciation for her moment in the spotlight. "And Mr. Bunny got a moose to keep him company."

"Yes, he certainly did," I agreed. "And we're also grateful for the presence of our new friend, Abe…"

"Shh! It's a secret," Susie and Abe said together. Susie's giggles mixed with Abe's wheezing, and I was wondering if he had had another glass of wine, but then he turned and gave me a wink.

I looked around to check for spies, in acknowledgment of this state secret, and then continued, "Abe's presence here tonight is part of one of the greatest miracles of our time, and perhaps any time: the arrival of neighbors from another world who came in peace and were welcomed in peace. We can all be grateful for living at a time that I don't think any of us…" and I looked at Susie "…will ever forget."

I sat down to amens from the adults and a loud burp from Elizabeth, when Abe put down his napkin and rose from his seat. "I don't know what your custom is for guests at Thanksgiving, but I just wanted to add a few words of my own. We have no holiday like this on Brogard, but we do share your belief in some sort of higher, organizing power in this universe. We teach our children that it's good manners to acknowledge gifts, whether they come from parents, friends, or from Ozu itself."

"Who's Ozu?" asked Sidney, keeping one eye on the kitchen door for the return of the turkey.

"That's the name those of us from the Western Continent give to that great power. I understand you have much the same thing here, with different names for God or Allah or the Supreme Being. We give thanks to Ozu. In the spirit of your holiday, then, I thank Ozu for bringing me to the Berman home, where I have been made to feel just like one of the family. And I thank all of you for the countless kindnesses you have shown me."

Abe sat down to silence. Elizabeth had dozed off, but the rest of us had been profoundly moved by this expression of faith and friendship. Well, almost all of us.

"Could someone pass the sweet potatoes?"

"Sure, Sid, let's eat."

Later that night, after the in-laws had gone home, the kids had been put to bed, and Larissa had called it a night, Abe and I sat downstairs where we had first gotten to know each other a little over a week ago. We each had a snifter with half an inch of Napoleon brandy in it, a foolish extravagance that I made a point of putting on my expense account. Just let Junior try to object.

"Abe, I was really touched by what you said at dinner this evening."

He started to turn—so help me!—a shade of purple from his cheeks to just above his gill flaps and it took me a moment to realize what I was seeing. Abe was blushing.

"Jake, your Earth customs are still new to me, but it seemed like an appropriate thing to do at the time. I hope I didn't overstep my bounds."

"Not at all, not at all. You really have become a part of the family. It's going to seem strange without you tomorrow, when we move you into the bungalow. Of course you're welcome back anytime… Susie wouldn't have it any other way."

Abe inhaled the aroma of the brandy, and then took a sip. "I have enjoyed talking and playing with her. Are all Earth children like that?"

I laughed as I put my snifter down. "No, our little Susie is a force of nature unto herself. When she was born, she rewrote the delivery, because she was 'sunny side up' and we ended up having to cut Larissa open to get her out."

Like many people, I had read the reports about Brogardi sexuality very carefully when they first appeared in the news. On that score, we really were remarkably alike. Apparently, the system worked.

"Sunny side up?"

"It means face up. She was facing a different direction than she was supposed to. She's been marching to the beat of a different drummer ever since," I told him, "You must have something special, Abe. She doesn't always warm up to strangers as quickly as she did to you."

"But then, I'm not your typical stranger."

"On the contrary, my friend, they don't come much stranger." I picked up the snifter for a sip, but noticed that Abe had that faraway look in his eyes he had had the first day. "Abe, you all right?"

"Jake, my friend, I am doing just fine." He stood, looking just the tiniest bit unsteady on his feet, and I remembered what he had said about our gravity being ever so slightly stronger than he was used to. "And now it's time to go to bed. Tomorrow is a big day. Thank you again, Jake. I think Junior chose wisely when he put me in your care."

Junior? When had he starting calling Graham by that name? I looked up, and saw Abe at the top of the stairs. He turned and put his fingers to his lips.

"Shh! It's a secret," he said, as he headed down the hall toward his room.

It Came from Outer Space

I hit the button signaling the projection booth to roll the film. On screen, we saw the familiar Graham Moose, followed by the interior of an old-fashioned movie palace. The lights dimmed on screen as the curtains opened. The movie within the movie showed black and white scenes from past decades of people hustling and bustling, technicians doing mysterious things with test tubes, and shadowy figures meeting in rich surroundings. There was no real story here, just images of purpose and activity.

A voiceover announcer, sounding very much in the period, breathlessly spoke, "Never in the history of motion pictures has the world been prepared for an entertainment event like this. Years in the making, featuring a cast of thousands. You'll thrill, you'll cry, you'll cheer. Graham Studios proudly presents the movie triumph of a lifetime."

The scene cut to a color shot of the modern exterior of a nondescript suburban home in early evening. "Coming soon to a theater near you will be the must-see movie of the year, starring…"

A different more contemporary voice replaced the original announcer. "Shh! It's a secret."

It cut to the Graham logo with the legend, "Coming next summer." Then the screen faded to black, with the darkness held a couple of beats longer than expected.

When the lights came up in the screening room, there was a moment of silence. Since it was only Junior and me in the room—the projectionist in his soundproof booth couldn't hear our discussion—there was no need for any posturing. Finally he looked at me. "Call me stupid, Jake, but I don't get it. It doesn't say anything."

I turned to Junior, "Like I told you, chief, not telling people anything is my specialty."

With Graham Studios taking a major roll of the dice on this project, he was not in the mood for any levity. "All this says is that we're releasing a big movie next year. Everybody already knows that. *Every* studio is releasing some kind of big film next year."

There were times when Junior showed moments of great insight, proving himself a worthy successor to his old man. This wasn't one of them. "Sly, if we told them what the secret was, all the other studios would know as well. What this trailer does is create a sense of mystery. Sure, we're all releasing big movies next year, same as we did this year, and last year, and the year before that. What's different is that this one is so big, we can't tell you anything about it, including its title."

"So how is this going to get us publicity?"

I reached into my pocket and handed him a laminated button. "It gets us publicity because we turn that lack of information into a selling point. We make people want to know what the big deal is."

Junior held up the button. It read, "Shh! It's a secret."

"When *Entertainment Weekly* and *Variety* call to ask what the gag is, we tell them it's no gag. We're not releasing *any* information on this one until its premiere. In fact, we might even consider getting you to do a few interviews where you refuse to answer any questions."

I looked at Junior. He was holding the button and considering it. "And that's going to drive them nuts." Bingo! He got it.

I merely smiled.

"Jake, that's brilliant. They're going to do our publicity for us. We don't confirm or deny any rumor about what the movie is or who's in it. We do the opposite of what everyone in town does for every other movie that gets released. By the time of the premiere, they'll be begging for information."

"That's what you pay me for."

"But what's this about next summer? I thought we were opening in May."

"With the 'summer movie season' stretching from the end of April to Labor Day, we can release it whenever we want. But by emphasizing 'summer' in the trailer, it will mean we won't attract undue attention when we plan the May opening."

Junior was clearly pleased. He was getting hyped on our hype. It was time to bring him back to reality.

"Play this right, and we could be the entertainment story of the year," I told him. "Now all you have to do is make the movie."

*   *   *

It was shortly before New Year's when the meeting convened in Junior's office. Abe was there, of course. I hadn't seen him in a couple of weeks, since he had gone back east to see his father. Since he was going to be out of circulation for the six weeks of intensive production, we thought it would minimize suspicions as to his whereabouts if everyone who might care where he was had a good long visit from him in December. So, just after he settled in on the lot, he took off again, giving our security people a chance to review procedures to make sure he could actually film in seclusion. Our secrecy campaign was starting to create a buzz, and one of the side effects was that the studio had had more gate crashers in the last two weeks than in the previous five years. Most of them were from the tabloids, to be sure, but they also included an enterprising freelancer from the *Wall Street Journal*.

Also present at the meeting was our director, Caroline Sosniak, who had done *Webbed Site* and been a favorite of Junior's ever since, and an elderly man who was unknown to me.

Abe was looking especially natty in his new clothes, with an open necked off-white shirt, double-breasted navy blue blazer, and sharply creased grey slacks. His blue skin looked positively dashing in this color-coordinated ensemble. He made a face at me when I walked in—the last to arrive—which the others interpreted as a sign of displeasure. Clearly, they hadn't spent much time with any Brogardi.

"Abe, it's great to see you. How was your trip?"

Abe rose from his seat next to THE DESK and walked halfway across the room to give me an embrace. Apparently, he had learned to act like the Earthans do, particularly in Hollywood. "Just wonderful, Jake. I had to see my father, of course, but otherwise I got to see the sights in New York City. Are you aware that Madison Square Garden is round, and doesn't contain any actual plant life?"

Before I could reply, Junior called the meeting to order. "We'll talk later," I said, taking my seat on the couch with Caroline. Next to her, slowly sinking into his chair, was the old man.

"Jake, we usually don't have you at script conferences, but because of your deep involvement in the project, I thought you ought to be here. You know Abe and Caroline, of course, but I don't think you've met Irving Moskowitz."

I stood up to shake hands with him. He had sunk deep into his chair, and I wanted to avoid having to watch him struggle to climb out of it, only to have to sit down again. I had to speak loudly and repeat my name, as Irving was a little hard of hearing.

Junior continued, "Irving's our writer."

"Really?" I asked. This guy looked like he had apprenticed writing title cards for Clara Bow movies. He should be enjoying his golden years, not writing the movie that could determine the fate of Graham Studios.

"Sly here thought he'd give a kid a break," Irving grunted. "I hope to make it big in the movies."

I wasn't sure if this was a joke for my benefit or not. "Irving worked for my dad years ago, and I wanted to keep this in the family," Junior said.

"Aren't you afraid—with all due respect, Mr. Moskowitz—that the script might lack a contemporary feel? After all, this is the first space alien story with a real space alien in it." I was beginning to wonder if Junior had lost his mind.

"Don't worry. Caroline is revising and polishing to make sure everything is right up to date. Right, Irving?"

"23 Skidoo, Sly." The old man then turned to me, and favored me with a wink.

Sly handed me the thick sheaf of papers bound by brass fasteners. Clearly, my input on the script wasn't desired or he would have sent this to me before the meeting. I could read it on my own time. I glanced at the cover memo summarizing the plot.

The Brogardi, as the film was still titled, told the story of a young Brogardi (Abe) who defied his parents to pursue a career on Earth in the movies. He has a platonic romance with an Earth woman—who would presumably be played by whichever of this year's up and coming stars we had under contract—and is eventually reconciled with his parents when he returns to them on the night of a big Brogardi festival. Apparently the romantic subplot would remain relatively chaste, because the verdict was still out from the scientists and doctors on whether humans and Brogardi could actually interrelate, so to speak.

This plot sounded awfully familiar. I looked at Irving. He beamed with satisfaction at being back in the saddle. "Abe's father, he wouldn't happen to be a cantor, would he?" I asked.

Irving winked at me again. "That's funny," he said, "You don't look bluish."

While the writer was trotting out hoary old plots that had been dated back in 1927—and even older jokes—I was stunned. What could they be thinking?

"Sly, I have some great ideas for casting here, but Al Jolson died years ago."

"What are you talking about? Jolson may have had a bad night, but he never died. They loved him." Irving was on a roll now. I wondered if he was going to start doing his whole vaudeville routine.

Junior either couldn't or wouldn't acknowledge the problem here. Security was one thing, but Irving's ancient shtick was not what we needed. Junior stood up behind THE DESK. Since it was also on a raised platform, this simple act served to stop all conversation dead in its tracks.

"What did you expect? Ray guns? We're making a simple family story, steeped in tradition."

Before I could raise any further objections, Caroline cut me off. "Jake, you're not here to critique, you're here to handle the publicity angle. And, as I'm sure I don't have to tell you, the hook here isn't the plot; it's the first movie starring a Brogardi. People will go for the novelty and, we hope, discover a star. It's my job to make this go down easy. If the story is old-fashioned, that means it will be that much more comfortable and familiar for the audience."

"I agree," said Abe, speaking up for the first time. "An old-fashioned Earth story is precisely what I want to do. I want to show everyone that I can be as good an actor as any Earthan."

Clearly, I had already lost this battle, but I gave it one last shot. "All right, make it easygoing and amiable, but who are you going to get to play Abe's parents? Where are you going to get all the extras for the big festival scene? How many Brogardi are you actually going to put in the cast? You think your father would like to be in the movie, Abe?"

Abe was about to answer, but Caroline cut us both off. "The other Brogardi will be played by humans."

"We're going to do it in blueface," chortled Irving, who by now had worn out his welcome with me.

"Don't you think that might be offensive to the Brogardi?"

"This movie is a showcase for Abe," said Junior. "The other Brogardi characters will be portrayed tastefully and respectfully, but the hook has got to be that he's the first Brogardi star."

Junior had spoken. The meeting broke up shortly thereafter. I wanted to speak to Abe, but Caroline spirited him off for some costume and camera tests. I had no desire to stick around with Irving, who was trying to pitch Junior on a remake of *Carmen Jones* with an all Brogardi cast. Junior didn't want to show his ancient employee any disrespect, but he had already served his purpose.

I don't know why the meeting had so bothered me. Caroline was right. The merits of the script were none of my concern. When the time came, my job was simply to promote the movie, and Abe's presence made it eminently promotable. I had sold many a second- and third-rate film. Maybe *The Brogardi* wouldn't be so bad.

Still, I had a queasy feeling.

Late that afternoon, I was in my office going over our winter release schedule, and making sure that each print had two trailers attached: one for the next one on the schedule, and the other one our teaser for *The Brogardi*. It was busywork, and I could have passed it off to an underling, but I needed to occupy myself. When the intercom buzzed, I was prepared to tell Betty to take a message, but then the door opened, and Abe sauntered in.

"Betty," I said into the speaker, "Hold my calls and call it quits for the day. Abe and I have some catching up to do."

I opened the office fridge and broke out a couple of bottles of a dark German beer I favored. "I hope you haven't overdosed on bubbles yet, Abe, because I think you'll find these especially flavorful."

Abe took a seat on the couch and put his feet up on my coffee table, resting them on a stack of *Daily Variety*. I first noticed his fine Italian shoes, remembering that Betty hadn't spared the expense account when it came to putting together Abe's wardrobe. I then noticed that he wasn't wearing any socks.

"They made my feet itch," he told me. "I'm more comfortable this way."

"Fair enough. In this town, anything eccentric in dress becomes a fashion statement. Who knows, maybe you'll start a trend. You could do for bare feet what John Travolta did for white suits."

"I'm afraid I don't get the reference."

I decided that Abe's education in the dark chapter of '70s pop culture known as "disco" would have to wait for another day. I was more interested to learn what he had been up to in the several weeks since I had seen him.

I sat on the lounge chair next to the couch, kicked off my shoes, and put my own feet up—in my case, on copies of the annual report of the conglomerate of which we were a small but profitable division. "Never mind about that, tell me about your trip to New York. You must have been glad to see your friends and family."

Abe made his displeased face. "Actually, except for my father, I didn't know anyone there, and I spent very little time with him. As ambassador, he has many obligations, you know."

He might have fooled most people, but I had gotten to know him as more than a gimmick for the next Graham picture. He wasn't merely blue skinned. He was blue.

"You sound as depressed as I feel," I said. "Couldn't your father make the time for you?"

"Oh, don't blame him. I had my own agenda of things to do. I wanted to see Earthan life," he said, smoothly changing the subject. "I went to a lot of Broadway shows, but I found them very confusing. I saw one called *Cats*, but it was cast entirely with humans. If they did a show called *Humans*, do you suppose all the parts would be played by cats?"

I suppose I found Abe's naïveté endearing, but his questions were usually quite logical. Given the curious mix of Brogardi-translated Earth lore he was working from, the gaps in his knowledge often led to surprising conclusions, but I never assumed it was a lack of intelligence at work. No doubt if I were to visit Brogardi, I'd be making the same sort of foolish errors, and it would be Abe who would have to indulge me.

I offered him another beer, snagging one for myself, and trying to figure out why I was in such a funk. Abe filled the awkward silence, and this time zeroed right in on the truth. "How's the family, Jake? Have Susan and Elizabeth grown much since I've seen them?"

"Elizabeth has learned how to roll, and is tearing around the house like a steamroller, while Susan is busting to tell everyone about her Brogardi friend. She misses you terribly." I think I did, too.

Abe took this all in. "I assume that as an adult, Larissa is still the same size?"

I laughed. "Larissa will appreciate your faith in her ability to stick to a diet during the holiday season."

"Yes, this is the time of your big festival season, is it not?"

"In fact, tomorrow night is New Year's Eve. What are your plans for the weekend?"

Abe pulled out a little calendar that he now carried along with his guidebook. "Other than a discussion with Caroline on Brogardi customs tomorrow morning, my schedule seems free and clear until next week."

I finished my beer and stood up, slightly wobbly. "Then pack your bags, Abe. You're coming home and celebrating the New Year in style."

His face broke out in his version of a big smile.

"Don't you think we ought to call Larissa? I seem to recall that she was rather upset at my surprise arrival last time."

I fixed him with a very serious look. "Shh! It's a secret."

We were both laughing—or, rather, I was laughing and Abe was wheezing—as we headed out to the parking lot.

Panic in the Year Zero!

"Can Susie come out and play?"

My joking shout as I arrived home brought a shriek of delight from elsewhere in the house.

"Daddy's home! Daddy's home!" I could hear her scampering from her room and down the hallway, racing to give me a big hug. Would I always engender that unconditional love? I was glad that the teenage years were still a long way off.

Susan took the turn at the bottom of the stair on two wheels—or five toes, if you're literal minded—and raced into my open arms. "Daddy, tomorrow night is New Year's, and Mommy said I can stay up past my bedtime to see the calendar change and… Eeeee!"

She had just noticed my guest. "Abe!" she shouted, at such a high pitch that every dog for blocks around must have gotten a splitting headache. Her dear old dad was instantly forgotten as she bounded over to Abe, and leapt into his arms, nearly knocking him over in the process.

"Easy, honey," I told her, "You'll have all weekend to play with Abe."

"Abe's having a sleepover? EEEEEEE!!!!!" This brought a new round of screams, as she jumped back down to inform her mother of this exciting turn of events.

This time I had hedged my bets. I had phoned her from the car as we pulled into the driveway. Thus, with all of two minutes' notice, a beaming Larissa came out to greet our visitor.

"Abe, it's so good to have you back again. We're so happy you're going to be joining us for New Year's."

"He's going to be here for New Year's? I get to stay up late with Abe? EEEEEEE!" It was starting to occur to me that my daughter was turning into the highly excitable type. You ever wonder what they do with all the caffeine they take out of decaf coffee? Apparently, they've been feeding it to Susie.

Larissa and Susan took Abe down to the guest room to settle him in, leaving me standing alone at the door.

"Hi, honey, I'm home," I said, to see if anyone would notice.

"Hello, Señor Berman," replied a somewhat startled Rosa, who had come out to see what all the commotion was about, and found me talking to myself in the entranceway.

The next day, I put in but a few hours at the studio, before dismissing the entire staff at lunchtime, so they could prepare for their various year-end revelries.

"Betty, do you have any big plans for this evening?"

She had just put the cover over her keyboard, and the matching slipcover over the computer deck and monitor. She was the only one I knew who did this besides my cousin Norm.

"Why yes, Mr. Berman, I do the same thing I've been doing for years. I get together with some friends for dinner, and reminiscence about old times."

How sweet. I imagined they'd toast the New Year around 9:30 and be fast asleep by 10.

"And I appreciate your letting me go early. I have to pack and be at the airport by four o'clock."

"The airport?"

"Why yes. Our party is in Las Vegas. After the show, we usually play blackjack until dawn. Last time I cleared ten thousand dollars. It was a nice way to start the New Year."

"I'm sure it was," was all I could manage to say.

"At least it would have been, if the pit boss hadn't accused me of being a card counter. Just for that, we're going to a different hotel this time."

I made a mental note to myself to refrain from asking Betty what her plans were for President's Day Weekend. I was afraid she might have a secret life serving as a mercenary paratrooper. "Have a Happy New Year, Betty," I told her.

"The same to you, Mr. Berman. I think this New Year will bring good fortune to us all."

The nice thing about being a highly paid studio executive was that I could easily afford to have other people prepare for our New Year's celebration. Rosa would be taking the night off, and we brought in an outside caterer to handle the food and the service. It was going to be a fairly intimate gathering, about twenty people, mostly family and some old friends. And Abe.

"Dear, how are we going to explain Abe to our guests without giving away your movie?" Larissa had asked me that morning. It was her most glaring fault: asking me a perfectly reasonable and obvious question. She usually did this when it was one that I had been trying to avoid in the hopes that it would go away if I ignored it long enough.

"Why not just say he's a long-lost relative… from your side of the family? It certainly would explain why you're so different from your parents."

"Very funny," she replied, fixing me with an expression that let me know that it wasn't funny at all. She continued to brush out her hair. "We've got to say something."

"Why not simply say that Abe was touring the studio on behalf of the Brogardi? When we learned he was alone for New Year's, we invited him to join our celebration?" It was plausible, it was simple, and it had the virtue of being nearly true.

"Are the Brogardi interested in Earth movies?"

"Nobody seems to know yet. The chief trade seems to be in high technology and medicine right now, but eventually we're going to start exporting DVD players and figure out how to adapt streaming video to their computer systems, and then they're going to need the content to go with them."

"Makes sense to me. Have you discussed this with Abe? It's his cover story, after all."

The problem resolved as far as she was concerned, Larissa completed her vigorous brushing and moved onto to the next item on the agenda, which had something to do with her eyebrows. The odd thing was that she would be spending a good portion of the day at some salon getting made up for tonight. I could've asked why she needed to do all this work that was simply going to be erased and redone, but I had gone down that path before and lived to regret it. My new philosophy regarding Larissa's actions was that if it didn't concern me, I shouldn't try to make any sense out of it.

Between Larissa and Betty and the two girls, I realized that my life was filled with women who seemed to be operating on a different plane of existence from me. Perhaps the aliens had landed a lot earlier than we realized.

On the trip back from the studio, I filled in Abe on his cover story. Strapped in beside me in a yellow turtleneck and dark blue pants, he was turning into quite the clothes horse. He agreed that the story made sense.

"If anyone asks, I can explain that we're studying Earth business methods to understand how our counterparts operate."

"Fine. It's a nice, boring explanation that no one should question too closely. If anyone gets too pushy, ask them what they know about double entry bookkeeping."

"What's that?"

"Doesn't matter. It's a great conversation killer." Abe pondered this for a bit. Traffic was moving at a crawl, and we were going to be sitting here for a while, so there was plenty of time to think. "Jake, if you don't mind my asking, how do you come up with stories like that?"

"Like what?"

"Like what I'm doing at the studio instead of making a movie?"

"I've been in public relations and publicity for twenty years. It's easy. The best lie is a partial truth. You leave out the parts you don't want anyone to know, and then reveal the rest. That way you don't have to remember whether you've told different people the same story or not. You just have to remember what you're not telling anyone." This was P.R. 101, but Abe looked at me as if I had revealed some dark and magical secret.

"You don't have a problem lying to people?"

"Well, Abe, there are lies and there are lies. If I tell people they're going to enjoy our animated holiday offering, *Santa's Smartphone*, everyone understands that's our intention, not our prediction. What I don't tell them is that we hope it's a hit because we have a lucrative licensing deal with a company that makes toy phones. No one cares because it's really beside the point."

"Do you lie to your family?"

I wasn't sure where he was going with this. "Not over anything important."

Now it was his turn to be confused. "How can you tell the difference?"

"Well, let me give you an example. When Susie was three, she spent all afternoon drawing a picture of the family. When she showed it to me, it was a page full of scribbles with three stick figures barely discernible through the layers of crayon. She asked me what I thought of it. What would you have said?"

"That it didn't look like your family, I suppose."

"You disappoint me, Abe. If I had done that, Susie would have burst into tears, ripped up the picture, and probably ended up spending years in therapy. Instead, I told her that I loved it, and I was going to take it to my office to show everyone."

"And did you?"

"Of course not. She was three. By the next day, she had done half a dozen more pictures, and forgotten all about her family portrait."

"So what was the point of lying?"

"It wasn't a lie, it was an expression of love. My daughter needed to hear that her efforts were appreciated by her Daddy, not receive a critique from an art historian. When I say I don't lie about anything important, I mean I don't cheat on my wife or promise to give Susie a pony when it's something I can't deliver."

Traffic had now come to a complete standstill. I hoped that the caterer had arrived before Rosa had left, because right now it looked like no one would be getting home for hours. Abe was again lost in thought.

"Don't the Brogardi have little white lies?" I asked him.

"Um, no," he replied, "Our culture is very strict about telling the truth or saying nothing at all. That's why I'm glad you've given me a story that is true. I'd hate to have to try out my acting talents on your guests."

The rest of the trip went uneventfully and, once we got off the highway, we were able to get home quickly. Abe mentioned that he'd begun working with an acting coach, and that the film would begin principal photography in mid-January.

"Nervous?" I asked.

Abe gave that simple question a good deal of thought. "I suspect that whether I answer that one 'yes' or 'no,' I'm going to be leaving out part of the story."

"I'll take that as a 'yes' *and* a 'no,'" I said, and that seemed to please Abe a lot.

*   *   *

Our New Year's parties were informal gatherings—by Hollywood standards at any rate. Guests milled around the house, eating, drinking, and going from conversation to conversation. Susie was running around in her pajamas, having a great time enjoying the rare privilege of life among the grown-ups. Several TV sets were on so that we could enjoy the countdown to the New Year in all four continental time zones, that being one of the many advantages of life on the Pacific Coast. Downstairs, the bartender had set up shop in the family room, and it was there that Abe was being cornered by my cousin Norm.

"The physics of the dimensional drive is simply astounding," he was informing Abe about his own planet's technology. "The equations are so elegant they brought tears to my eyes. Did you have much to do with it?"

Abe had decided to experiment with vodka this evening, and was having a Russian concoction that was flavored with vanilla beans. "Other than being a passenger, I'm afraid not," he told Norm. "My studies were elsewhere."

Norm lit up. Could he be getting in on the ground floor of the next cutting edge Brogardi technology?

"Really?" he said, trying and failing to be nonchalant. "Tell me about your studies."

"There isn't that much to tell. I specialized in the music of the Southern Continent during its formative years. They spent several of your centuries using a strictly limited, five-tone scale for all their musical compositions. It was excruciatingly and profoundly mind-numbing."

Norm was crestfallen, but having brought up the subject, he had to see it through to the end. "What did you conclude?" he asked, skipping to the last chapter of the book.

"There's no accounting for taste," Abe noted succinctly. "It's one of the many reasons I was eager to come to Earth. I find our differences as staggering as our similarities."

It was time to rescue Abe from Norm—and perhaps vice versa. I set the Susie missile to stun and fired it at Abe.

"Happy New Year!" she shouted as she ran up to Abe, making it sound as if it was the first time the occasion had ever been noted. In a way, she was right—it was the first time she would be celebrating it. She noticed Norm, and repeated her greeting. He gave her a friendly wave and moved on, looking for more challenging conversational partners.

"Look, Daddy, it's almost New Year's." I looked where Susan was pointing. On the TV screen, Times Square in New York was packed with people celebrating the countdown. Everyone stopped to watch the countdown, then went back to what they were doing: the old year had another three hours to go, here.

"Actually, sweetheart, it's just New Year's on the East Coast. I explained it all to you before. It won't happen here until midnight."

"So we're still in the past?"

I gave Abe a knowing look. "I'm afraid so, Susie."

"Then I'm going to see what year it is in my bedroom. Mr. Bunny is all confused." Susan raced up the stairs to the main hallway. When I turned back to Abe, the bartender was pouring him another drink.

"This is really quite interesting," he said, taking a sip. "I wasn't aware that your alcohol could be sweet."

"Oh, I can get you drinks much sweeter than that, but you ought to take it easy. The night's still young."

We headed out to the patio. The evening was unseasonably warm, even for Southern California. We might even be able to go swimming tomorrow, I thought.

"Do you have holidays like this back home?" I asked Abe, who was staring somewhat wistfully at the night sky. I didn't even know if you could see his star system from Earth. My ignorance of things Brogardi was really astounding. I resolved to do something about it—next year.

"You mean 'Hurrah! We're Changing the Calendar!' holidays? No, mere numeric progression was never the focus of much activity on Brogard, although there was one group that use to have quite a festival around the midpoint of the year, under the theory that the hard work was over, and it was downhill the rest of the way."

"Sounds like a fun holiday. Perhaps we should plan our next vacation around it." We both turned at the voice, and saw Larissa had come out to join us.

"I'm afraid you wouldn't find them much fun," said Abe, "They all died out about three thousand years ago. They made the worst music, too. Remind me never to play it for you."

"You must find our ways somewhat bewildering," I offered, stretching out on one of the deck chairs. I had flicked on the underwater pool lights, so that the water lit up without taking away from the grandeur of the starry night.

Larissa sat at the foot of the lounge, while Abe leaned against the edge of the deck. "Actually," said Abe, "my guidebook is silent on one point, which usually suggests it's something you Earthans are sensitive about."

"You're among friends, Abe," said Larissa.

"Well, if I understand this correctly, you number your years from the birth of one of your Earthan deities, correct?"

"That's right. We count the years as B.C.—before Christ—or A.D.—which stands for 'Anno Domini,' Latin for 'year of our Lord.'"

"All right, then, but didn't you just celebrate his birthday last week? So why would you mark your years off from a week *after* his birth?"

"Well, Jesus was Jewish. Maybe we're celebrating his circumcision."

Larissa swatted me. "It has to do with the way the calendar was developed. New Year's used to come in March. As late as the mid-18th century it was still celebrated in March in England, when they finally switched from the Julian to the Gregorian calendar."

I looked at her strangely. "How do you know this stuff?"

"If I told you, I wouldn't be able to maintain my sense of mystery."

Abe drained his glass. "I'm afraid some Earthan customs are just going to elude me. No wonder Mr. Bunny is confused."

"So what do you celebrate? I can't believe the Brogardi don't have any holidays." This was probably how Larissa collected this information. She'd file it away, and spring it on someone else months from now, and they'd be amazed at how she seemed to know everything.

"We tend to celebrate events rather than cycles. The selection of a new ruler. The completion of schooling. The birth of a child."

"We were having a party for the birth of Elizabeth the day your father arrived. We're not so different."

"No," allowed Abe, "but next year, I wouldn't be surprised if many Earthans celebrated the anniversary of his arrival. For us, it will simply be a matter of history."

The patio doors whooshed open, and Susan padded out onto the deck. "Mommy, Daddy, Abe! It's almost New Year's!"

I looked at my watch. It was nearly 10 o'clock.

* * *

By the time midnight actually rolled around, Susie was fast asleep. I tried waking her up, but after saying, "Happy New Year, Daddy," she went right back to dreamland.

At the stroke of the new year, Larissa and I kissed, the same as we had started each year in the nearly two decades I had known her. "You better find Abe," she said as we broke the clinch. "He doesn't have anyone to kiss."

"Sorry, dear. That's where I draw the line. My loyalty to the studio only goes so far."

She glanced around the upstairs living room, where we had both migrated over the course of the evening, and stopped short. "I guess I was wrong."

I turned to see what she was looking at. It was Abe, entwined in a tight embrace with Jo Heiden, a colleague of Larissa's. Jo was the classic blonde bombshell, and tonight she had dressed the part. She was in a silver lame outfit consisting of a clinging, short skirt, and a top that appeared to be little more than a large napkin tied around her neck and waist. It left very little to the imagination, and she appeared to be encouraging Abe to discover the rest. I hesitated to interrupt, but since Jo's husband was also attending the party, I figured I owed it to Junior to avoid a scene, if not to Abe.

"Abe, I've been looking all over for you. There's someone I wanted you to meet." Jo's expression flashed from being startled to one of annoyance, "Happy New Year, Jo. I think I saw Rob downstairs with your coat."

She easily called my bluff as she simultaneously beat a retreat. "I didn't wear a coat," she said, turning to Abe and pressing a finger to his lips. "Don't forget my offer, babe." We both watched her depart. I hoped Abe would forgive me. If I was Abe, I wouldn't have.

"Her offer?" I asked, giving him one of those sly "just among us guys" looks.

"I wanted to ask you about that. I'm working on my colloquialisms but she came up with one—at least I assume it is—that I hadn't come across before. She said she wanted to make it with me."

"And?"

"She wouldn't tell me what it was that she wanted to make. You use the word for everything from cooking to art to manufacturing, but none of them seemed appropriate."

Putting my arm around his shoulders, I took him off to a quiet corner. "Yes, it's colloquial, all right. She was offering to have sex with you."

"Ah, yes, I get it now. That would explain it."

Now it was my turned to be puzzled. "Explain what?"

"Why she was so interested in the size of my body parts. It was a most peculiar conversation. She seemed quite surprised when I told her about—"

"Abe? Let's not go there, all right? There are some things that friends just don't discuss with each other."

"Really?"

We had never gotten onto this topic, and Abe clearly was as confused about our customs as I was about his. "Let's save it for another day, okay?"

"Sure, Jake, but I did have a question about something else we had talked about. Did you say that Jo has a husband?"

"Yeah, he's a real estate attorney. About as exciting as watching cement set. I saw him about half an hour ago, snoring away on one of the deck chairs."

"Well, if she was offering to have sex with me, would she have to lie to her husband about it? And if she did, would that be one of those acceptable 'white lies' you were telling me about?"

What a way to start the year. "Have a seat, Abe," I said, motioning to the couch. "The short answer is that it's not acceptable, and married people who care about each other don't do such things. The long answer may take a while."

Abe pulled out his pad. "Should I be taking notes?"

"I don't think that will be necessary."

By 2 A.M., the guests had gone, Susan was tucked in with Mr. Bunny, Elizabeth was looked in on, and Abe had retired to his room—alone. I was already in bed, while Larissa puttered around the room doing the dozens of mysterious things she felt obliged to do each evening before she, too, could get into bed.

I told her the story of Jo's propositioning Abe. "And I think the moral is that we cross her off any guest list for the duration," I concluded.

"How do you know Abe wasn't coming on to her?" Larissa demanded. I looked at her without answering. "Well, it's possible. He's a single, adult, male. Who knows what his sex drive is like? Do you?"

"I can honestly say that I don't."

"Well, I keep seeing all these news stories that they're just like us. Maybe he's lonely. Maybe he needs to get laid."

I sat up in bed. "Now hold on there, I've been called many things in my line of work but 'pimp' is not one of them."

Larissa came over and sat on the bed. "No, no, no. I didn't mean that it was your responsibility. It's just that he's an adult. It's not up to you to protect him like he's your child."

"And just think of the publicity possibilities: Mad rapist from the stars toplines in latest Graham family feature. We should sell a lot of tickets on the curiosity value alone."

"Well, Junior didn't take a vow of celibacy before he got married two years ago. I don't see why Abe should."

She had a point. What's more, all this talk had been giving me ideas as well. I reached over and turned off the lights, and then greeted the new year with my wife in the privacy of our bedroom.

And, heaven help me, I kept flashing on images of Abe and Jo—sans napkin—while we were doing so.

I slept until late morning, then padded out to the dining room in my robe and slippers, to discover that everyone else was already awake and greeting a beautiful new day. It was several degrees warmer than usual, and a disturbingly perky Rosa had set up a breakfast buffet on the patio. As a rule, I didn't like seeing anyone that full of life until I had at least splashed water on my face and poured a cup of coffee down my throat.

Elizabeth was sitting in her stroller, slurping on a bottle, while Larissa and Susan were in bathing suits, sitting on the edge of the pool, just getting their feet wet.

"Good morning, ladies," I called. "Where's Abe?"

"He's showing us how long he can stay underwater," shouted Susan.

I walked over to the edge of the pool. There, at the bottom of the deep end, wearing a pair of Ducklings swim trunks, sat Ambassador Gezunt's little boy. He looked up at me and waved, but otherwise remained seated.

"He said he wanted to see how his gills worked in Earth water," Larissa said, as she stood to kiss me. Leaning in close, she breathed into my ear, "Just think of what Jo could make of that."

"Yes," I harrumphed, "Just a typical morning at the Berman household."

"Go have your coffee, dear, and change into your bathing suit."

I waved at Abe, and headed back to the bedroom.

I felt much better after washing up, changing, and getting my caffeine fix. When I returned outdoors, Abe was out of the pool and having a bowl of fresh fruit. Susan and Elizabeth were playing on a blanket in the shade, with the baby turning into quite the aggressive "peek-a-boo" player. It was nice to see my two girls getting along.

"Where's Larissa?"

"She went to get me a spray bottle," replied Abe. "Did you know that you have chlorine in your water?"

"Yes, of course. I put it in myself. It kills the algae and bacteria that might grow."

"Another peculiar Earthan custom, I suppose. I need some fresh water to get rid of the stinging in my gills." Larissa came out with the spray can she used for shpritzing her plants, and handed it to Abe. He began spraying himself around the throat. "That's much better."

I watched in fascination. "Where do you swim on Brogard, if you don't have swimming pools?"

"Who said we don't have pools? We just build them next to streams, so that we have a constant supply of fresh, running water."

"Don't you end up with fish in your pool? Or don't you have any aquatic life on Brogard?"

"Besides myself?" Abe wheezed a bit, enjoying his own little joke. "Yes, but a simple screen can keep the water flowing while keeping the various wildlife away. Of course there was the time when the screen came off after a big storm, and the pool was filled with—"

"*Mommy! Daddy! Elizabeth fell in the pool!*"

My heart froze. Susan screamed and pointed at the pool, where Elizabeth had rolled off the deck and into the deep end. Before either Larissa or I could move, Abe leapt out of his chair and dove into the water. Time seemed to shift into slow motion as we followed Abe's path to the pool. I saw his blue form cutting through the water, but I couldn't figure out where Elizabeth was.

Suddenly, a fountain of water gushed up, with two blue arms holding a shrieking, crying baby in the center of it. Larissa grabbed Elizabeth as I helped a coughing, sputtering Abe out of the pool.

"Abe saved the baby! Yay!" Susan was running around the deck out of sheer excitement and a lack of any other way to participate. Abe coughed some more, and pointed at the table.

"Susie, get me the spray bottle," I said, as Abe indicated that that was what he wanted.

Larissa wrapped Elizabeth in a towel, and hurried into the house. I handed Abe the spray, and then followed in after her. I saw the room was empty as my eyes adjusted to the relative darkness indoors, and I couldn't figure out where she had gone. Then I heard the baby crying, and followed the howls to her bedroom.

"How is she?" I gasped, as I raced in.

"She... she's fine," said an equally breathless Larissa. "She's soaking wet and she swallowed some water, which she's now spit up, along with most of her breakfast, but she's okay." Larissa was stripping her out of the sopping wet clothes and diaper, and making "there, there" noises at her.

"Are you okay?"

"I don't know. Let me deal with this crisis, and then I'll figure it out."

I went over and put my arm around her. "Eight o'clock tomorrow morning, I'm calling the contractor to install the babyproof fencing on the deck. I'd call today if I thought I could get them. I don't know why I put it off. If something happened to her, I'd never forgive myself."

A now-recovered Elizabeth had cried herself into exhaustion, and was drifting off to sleep. Her parents would be having nightmares for a week, but she looked as peaceful as could be. Larissa put her down in the crib, checking the rail locks twice before being convinced, and we headed downstairs together.

We found Abe and Susan standing in the living room, looking upstairs as we came down. Larissa went over and gave them each a hug. "My heroes," she said, then sat down on the floor and began to cry. I took in the scene, and I began to cry, too.

Happy New Year, indeed.

The Man Who Fell to Earth

January is usually a busy month, as we're finalizing the plans for our release schedule for the year. Betty returned from Vegas only two thousand dollars richer—I suspected she really was a card counter, and was trying to throw off suspicion—and had an autographed picture of Tom Jones on her desk. "Betty," it read, "You're quite a gal. Love, Tom." I resolved not to ask her about it. My life was already too complicated.

"It's good to be working again, Mr. Berman," she greeted me on her first morning back. Yes, I suppose it was, if you were a sorceress or an international spy or whatever she really was, but the whole experience with Elizabeth had soured me in a way from which I had still not recovered. Naturally, we weren't advertising the fact that we were such inept parents that we needed rescuers from space, so no one knew why I was in such a foul mood.

Even as we profusely showered Abe with our undying gratitude, I think he understood that something had changed, and he was ready to move back into his bungalow the next morning. He was tied up learning his lines and rehearsing with his acting coach, so we didn't see each other for the next few weeks.

I was meeting with the head of the art department to go over the proposed poster art for some upcoming releases when Betty buzzed that I had a call from one of the sets. Given the volatility of the egos involved, I always interrupted whatever I was doing to deal with the potential catastrophe. Nine times out of ten it was nonsense, but if someone felt they had to call me from the set, I didn't want to have to explain to Junior why I was too busy the time it turned out to be an actual emergency.

"This is Jake."

"Jake, it's Abe. When are you going to come down to see me work?"

I saw Betty's fine hand here. She knew something had happened over New Year's that I didn't want to talk about, and she knew me too well to figure I'd deal with it in my own time. In fact, I was once again hoping that anything I ignored would eventually go away.

"Hello, Abe," I replied somewhat cautiously. "I've been busy with the art department planning our summer campaigns. How are you doing?"

"Just fine, just fine. But I've missed seeing you," he said somewhat plaintively. How could he understand why I was so withdrawn, when I didn't understand it myself? "Look, they're signaling they want me back on the set, but I want you to come down this afternoon and watch us shoot. This acting stuff is a lot of fun."

"I'm sure it is, but I'm up to my ears in work…"

"No excuses. After we shut down for the day, you and I can go back to my place. You haven't seen my bungalow since the day you dropped me off here."

He was right. I was avoiding him, and it was entirely my fault. "All right, Abe. I think I can be down there about four. Is that all right?"

"That's great. I can't wait to see you."

I knew I could wait. I just didn't know if I could explain why.

If you've never been to a movie set, you probably imagine it as quite glamorous. The stars all sipping champagne and nibbling on caviar between takes, or perhaps slipping off to their dressing rooms for athletic sexual encounters. The reality is quite different. You'd be better off imagining a construction site. The red light signaling that film was rolling was off, so I slipped onto the darkened sound stage, picking my way over cables, equipment, and furniture. Except for the set where the scene was being shot, it looked like a not especially orderly warehouse.

One of the assistant directors ran over to see who the interloper was, but backed off immediately when I told him, "Tell Caroline one of the suits is on the set." The so-called creative people referred to those of us who actually ran the business as "the suits," to separate us from those people who worked purely for the aesthetic enjoyment of sharing their artistic vision with the world. That, and as much as their agent could squeeze out of us for salary, perks, and profit participation. Caroline, being a veteran, was into us for gross points, meaning she'd be taking her cut out of the first dollars the studio earned. Abe, a mere novice, had been offered, in addition to his hefty salary, part of the net profits, an ephemeral figure that would probably never be achieved. There was a reason such deals were referred to as "monkey points." Anyone with more intelligence than a monkey realized they'd be unlikely to see a dime on the back end.

Caroline was dressed in the *de rigeur* directorial garb of baggy pants, baggy shirt, and baggy jacket. In the reverse Hollywood pecking order, the director ranked higher than the stars because she (or he) *didn't* have to look attractive. Caroline was being paid for her brains, not how she'd look on three thousand screens opening weekend. As befitted her position as the empress of the set, she resented my appearance. This was her domain, and the arrival of one of the suits could only be a challenge to her authority.

I raised my hands in supplication. If I had a white cloth to show I was under a flag of truce, I would have waved it. "I'm here at Abe's request. He wanted me to come down and take a look. It probably wouldn't hurt for me to see what's going on in terms of planning future publicity, but I'm strictly an observer."

"No sweat, Jake. You can take my seat." Now that she had established who was in charge, she could afford to be magnanimous. By letting me sitting in her director's chair, she was acknowledging me as a visiting potentate who deserved respect. I appreciated the generosity. There were some directors who suddenly discovered technical problems that brought production to a screeching halt whenever any of the "suits" arrived on the set. Naturally, these problems were instantly solved the moment they left.

Caroline headed across to where Abe was sitting in what looked like a theater dressing room. He was at the mirror, adjusting a wig on his head. They were shooting the scene where his character sees his mother for the first time since he has become an actor. Since he was the only authentic Brogardi in the cast, his parents were humans in elaborate blue makeup. Marjorie Grange, the veteran character actress who played his mother, had even had all her own hair shaved off to play the part with greater authenticity.

"All right, let's run through this and then we're going to do a take. Abe, you're overjoyed to see your mom. Marj, you're thrilled to see your boy, but you're not sure you understand what he's doing. Got it?" They both nodded. "And, action."

Abe took off the wig and rubbed some cream on his scalp as Marjorie entered the dressing room. She was attired in some garb that presumably was typical Brogardi clothing. At least I hoped it was. This was too important a film to try to finesse such easily checkable details.

She looked at him in confusion. "Yekl, my son, is it really you?"

"Mother, when did you arrive on Earth?" He stood and turned, and they put out their hands and touched palms. Is that how Brogardi expressed affection? All this hugging and kissing must be driving him up the wall.

"Your father and I arrived when we got your message that you would not be home for your sister's graduation festival. Your father was devastated."

Abe paused, and looked at her. "You mean... he's here? At the theater?"

"No, he refused to come. He's sitting in a hotel room, saying that you will rejoin your family, or leave it for good. Yekl, you must come home."

"And... cut! Abe that was wonderful, we're going to use that take." Caroline ran over and patted him on the back. "Marjorie, you were right on the money. Try not to cry, though, it might streak the makeup."

"Wait, I thought that was a rehearsal," said Abe.

"I always film the rehearsal. What if you give a great performance and I miss it? Now I'm covered either way." She turned to the crew. "Set up for the closeups, and then we'll wrap for the day."

It would take several minutes for the lights and cameras to be moved for the closeup takes, first of Abe and then of Marjorie, trying to recapture the same feeling as they redid the scene. If things were going this smoothly, it was no wonder Junior felt we could be in post-production by the beginning of March and ready with a release print by May. Abe moved off the set and, as he stepped out of the glare of the bright lights, spotted me in the director's chair. "Jake, my friend. You made it." As I stood up, he jogged over and grabbed me in a big bear hug.

"Good to see you, too," I gasped. "I think you've left one of my ribs intact."

"I'm just so pleased you're here," he said, putting me down.

"Abe, why didn't you tell us about the way Brogardi greet each other? All that bodily contact must be unusual for you."

"It certainly was," he wheezed, "at least at first. Now I love it. But we're going for authenticity here, and a good Brogardi son doesn't clamber all over his parents the way your children do."

Geez, how did he put up with Susan all that time? "You should have told us. We would have told Susie it's not polite."

"Nonsense. Then we both would have been unhappy. Like I keep saying, Jake, I find our differences much more interesting than our similarities."

An attractive young woman in a striped shirt and worn jeans sauntered over. She had flowing red hair, stunning eyes, and the sort of full curves that had become stylish again. Not quite Rubenesque, but it was clear this woman had never worried about anorexia.

"Jake, I want you to meet Linda Reid. She's plays my manager."

Ah, this year's up-and-coming starlet. "Pleased to meet you, Linda. I'm Jake Berman, the senior vice president for publicity."

"Oh, I know who you are, Mr. Berman."

"You do? And please, it's Jake."

She flashed me the winning smile that probably had landed her the part. "Of course I do, Jake. Abe hasn't stopped talking about his good friend who's been introducing him to Earth family life."

I looked at Abe. "Oh, you have? I hope we won't be reading about this in the trades…"

"Oh, don't worry," interrupted Linda. "Everyone on the set has signed a secrecy agreement. We all know how important this film is going to be, and don't want to do anything to screw it up for Abe."

The assistant director came over and ignored me and—amazingly—Linda. "Abe, you're wanted back on the set for your closeup."

"Jake, we should be done in about twenty minutes. Don't run off."

"I'm here for the duration," I said.

"Well, I'm not," said Linda. "I've got an early call in the morning. Pleased to meet you, Jake." She gave me a warm handshake and a warmer smile. "See you tomorrow, Abe," she added, giving him a peck on the cheek.

Before I could even figure out what had happened, she was gone, and Abe was back on the set.

Abe had no reason to feel cheated if *The Brogardi* never showed any net profits. One of the reasons was that everyone who had to do anything for him—myself included—spared no expense in making him comfortable. That all added to the costs that would have to be recovered, many times over, before any imaginary profits would ever be realized, but it also meant that while he was a guest of Graham Studios, Abe would live like a king. At least like an Earth king. I had no idea what a Brogardi king lived like, or if they even had one. I really did have to get after Betty to provide me with some background materials.

His bungalow consisted of a large living room/dining area, backed by a fully functional kitchen and, to my surprise, a working bar. Off to the back was the bedroom and bathroom, but what caught my eye coming in was the large home entertainment center that had been set up. Stacks of DVDs and even some old videocassettes lay strewn about, so the equipment was clearly getting a good workout. I followed Abe over to the bar, where he showed me he had three kinds of beer on tap.

"I mentioned to Dick that I liked beer…"

"Dick?"

"Dick Lyman, your operations chief. He told me I hadn't lived until I had a black and tan. Have you ever had one?"

I was too stunned to reply. What sort of monster were we creating? We had hired Abe to bring Brogardi authenticity to the film, and he was turning into one of the boyos.

Abe expertly drew down the stout and ale into large pint glasses, and handed me one. "*L'chaim*," he said, clinking my glass, then downing enough to lower the foamy head an inch or two.

"*L'chaim*? Who taught you that?"

"Irv. He was down on the set for some rewrites."

"Well, I see you've been well taken care of," I said, sitting down on one of the bar chairs.

Abe came around from the bar and took the other seat. "Jake, I'm not sure what the Earth protocol is on this, so I'm just going to trust my Brogardi instincts and be honest. You've been very distant since New Year's, and I'm wondering if I did something wrong."

I sighed. Every time I tried to run away from a problem, the world conspired to make me face it. Here it was, and there was no avoiding it.

"You're right, Abe. And it's not your fault. To the contrary, it's my fault." I took a sip of beer, knowing that once I said this, I would never be able to hide from it again. "To tell you the truth…"

"Please."

"I was ashamed."

"But, Jake, why on Earth or Brogard did you have any reason to be ashamed?"

"First, because I was so negligent that my baby girl almost drowned, and second, because I'm such a failure as a father that when the moment for action came, I was frozen in place. You were the one who saved her, not me. And every time I look at you, I'm reminded of my own inadequacy." I was on the verge of weeping. I supposed I'd have to ask Junior to assign someone else to take care of Abe. Clearly, I was unfit to continue.

I felt a hand on my shoulder. "Jake, I don't pretend to fully understand Earth psychology, but logic tells me you're wrong on both counts."

"How so?"

"Well, didn't Larissa say that that was the first time Elizabeth had started crawling? You had no reason to know she could move that quickly and that directly. And didn't you call the builders the next morning to install the safety fence, so that it could never happen again?"

"That still doesn't explain why I didn't move. If you weren't there, a guard rail after the fact wouldn't have mattered."

"Jake, look at me."

I glanced at him. "Yeah?"

"No, really look at me. What are these things on my neck?" He turned so I couldn't miss his gills. "The way Earthans developed from apes, our ancestors came from the seas. It was sheer instinct. A few moments later, you would have done the same thing, and still been there in plenty of time."

I didn't want to believe him, but he was making a lot of sense. I took a long swallow of beer, as much to clear my throat as anything else. "I've been beating myself up over this for weeks. That's why I've been avoiding you and all thoughts of the movie."

"Aren't you glad we spoke? To speak with great truthfulness to a friend is a great precept among us. You have honored me with your candor."

"If acting like a fool is an honor. Abe, you saved my daughter's life. It's something I can never repay."

Abe gave that odd grimace that passed for a smile. "There's an old Brogardi saying that may lose something in the translation, but it seems apt. It goes: friends don't need bookkeepers. Does that make sense?"

"Indeed," I said, raising my glass to him. "Let me give you an Earth teaching in return: if a person saves a life, it is as if they have saved a whole world."

"I don't understand."

"Well, suppose Elizabeth grows up and one day discovers the cure for the common cold? Or one of her children turns out to be a gifted musician, or her grandchild becomes a great leader. None of those things could ever have happened if you hadn't saved her."

"But they may not happen, anyway."

"True, there are no guarantees. But thanks to you, now we'll have the chance to find out."

Abe pondered that for a moment. "That's very nice, Jake. I like that a lot." He looked at our glasses. "And it's time for a refill." He went behind the bar and went to work, while I walked over to the TV area and examined what movies he'd been watching in his off hours. They were nearly all old science fiction movies featuring alien invasions, usually with bug-eyed monsters threatening our womenfolk or, in the later ones, being cut to ribbons by our womenfolk. There was enough here for several day-long marathons featuring the xenophobic people of Earth running in fear and horror from the most horrible monsters Hollywood, Tokyo, or elsewhere could imagine. The final reel almost always had them slaughtered in a genocidal counterattack that took no prisoners.

"Um, you know, Abe, these films don't exactly put Earth in the best light. I'd be happy to recommend some titles that are more, er, uplifting."

Abe wheezed in amusement, "Not to worry. I understand that this is all just…"

He seemed to be stumbling for the word. "Make believe?" I suggested.

"Exactly," he said, apparently greatly relieved. "I'm finding it very recreational."

"You know, Abe, we have screening rooms here. If you'd like, I can get the films, and you can see them on a really big screen. You don't have to sit here alone in your room and—"

"Oh, no," he replied quickly, "This is just fine. I prefer being able to, uh, study them on my own." He came over with the fresh black and tans. "I'm having a great time, and I have you to thank for it."

"*L'chaim*, Abe."

"*L'chaim*, Jake."

E. T.

One of the mogul traditions that Graham Senior had established at his studio—and that Junior annoyingly continued—was summoning people to meetings at the most embarrassing and inconvenient places. One legendary studio chief had even conducted high-level business meetings while sitting on the toilet, demonstrating not only that his time was so valuable he didn't have a moment to waste, but that he was so powerful that everyone else would have to meet him on his terms, no matter how uncomfortable. Junior, fortunately, didn't go that far, but he did maintain a sauna on the studio grounds. It was supposedly open for everyone to use, but only seemed to be in operation when he wanted to remind someone of who was boss. Today, it was my turn for that reminder.

I stripped down in the locker room, and wrapped myself in the towels provided by the attendant. This was someone with easily the softest job at the studio, since most days he had nothing to do. It was a spot usually, but not always, filled by someone from Junior's extended family. From the piles of books on his desk in the corner of the locker room, I guessed he was some nephew working on his thesis and happy for the income. Give Junior this: in acknowledgment that this whole thing was a power trip, a large sign over the desk warned, "No tipping!" Junior took care of his own, and we weren't to feel obligated any further.

Junior was already in there, and the enclosed room had become exceedingly hot. Either I was merely one of a string of people paying a call, or he really liked it in there. Since I was never down here unless summoned, I didn't know.

I took a seat on the upper of the hard wooden benches that ran on two decks around three sides of the sauna. I would have liked to get right to the point of the meeting and gotten the hell out of there, but that's not the way this game was played. We had to wait a sufficient amount of time, until my pores were deemed sufficiently open—"sweating out the poisons" was the way he put it—before we could begin. I was on the verge of dozing off when I heard my name from somewhere off in the haze.

"Glad you could make it, Jake. I wanted to discuss the *Brogardi* premiere with you." Pleasantries, yet. We could have done this in five minutes over the phone, or ten in his office. What with the shower and rubdown—it was all part of the package—this little discussion was going to bite two hours out of my afternoon. Oh, well, it was his dime we were on.

"You'll pardon me for not bringing any notes," I offered, waving my hands at the towels. I wondered if that was one of his reasons for these meetings: no cue cards.

"Caroline tells me that they're more than halfway through production, and they should wrap by the beginning of March."

"Caroline was down here?"

Junior laughed. "No, this is one of the last of the sex-segregated hideaways." Lucky Caroline. "That's still two months of post-production," I noted.

"Less," countered Junior, "We're going to speed up post, with a team of editors working around the clock. Other than the usual stuff, like looping and recording the score, there won't be much more to do. It's not like we need a lot of special effects, eh?"

"Okay, so that takes us to late April or early May. What's the game plan?"

"Well, I want a big gala premiere sometime in May, so that we can platform it the following week, and then go wide for the Memorial Day Weekend."

"Platform it? Why bother opening it in just a few cities? This isn't a picture that's going to need word of mouth to get it going."

Junior leaned toward me. "No, but we want to make this a special event. The demand should be at a fever pitch by the time the film opens locally. We haven't platformed a major release in years."

"We haven't had to. Everyone rolls the dice on opening weekend now."

"If we can get the premiere for the second week of May, then by Memorial Day, we will own the box office."

Junior seemed sure of himself, but I remained skeptical. He was thinking like the big boys now, and we simply didn't operate in that league. "It's a risk, Sly. If the premiere fizzles, that's two weeks for everyone to lose interest in the film. I think we should go from premiere to the widest possible opening immediately."

"Jake, don't worry about it. That decision has already been made. What I want you to concentrate on is the premiere." Junior leaned back with a sigh. I was hoping that meant he had now imparted the information he could have sent in a two line memo, and I could begin the process of extracting myself from this ninth circle of hell.

"You're the boss. Where do you want the premiere? The Chinese Theater? The Dome?"

"New York, Jake. I want you to get us Radio City Music Hall, and make this the movie premiere of all time."

No one could complain Junior didn't dream big. "Ah, Sly? Don't you think that's going to draw attention to our project?"

"That's exactly why I'm putting you in charge. Keep the lid on it until we're ready to go. Money's no object." Uh oh, famous last words.

"Really?"

Junior realized what he had said. "Well, within reason, of course. But if you have to go a little overboard this time, this is the one to do it on. Keep me posted on your progress. I have some other plans once you have this part locked down."

Given the time difference, it was already too late to call the East Coast and check if the facility was even available on this short notice. I promised Junior I'd attend to it first thing in the morning.

"Excellent. I knew you were the right one for this job," he said, standing up. "Let's head to the showers. I'm really going to enjoy that massage now."

I let him precede me, and took my time getting to the stalls. Even at this salary, they couldn't pay me enough to shower with the boss.

As I was examining myself in the mirror, Ben, Junior's masseuse, came over to say hello. "I understand you're working on that big hush-hush project for Mr. Graham."

I smiled noncommittally.

"Well, when you see Abe again, tell him I said hello. He hasn't been down for his regular massage for over a week, and I'm wondering if he's finally gotten used to Earth gravity."

Ben wandered off to check on Junior's progress, and I looked after him, not quite sure if I had heard that right. Abe appeared to be going native even more than I had previously thought.

Later that afternoon, I was back at my desk, trying to catch up when the phone rang. It was Diane, one of my assistants, whose job it was to review all the clippings of reviews and stories about Graham films. She was in a state of panic.

"Calm down, Di. It can't possibly be as bad as all that."

"It's worse. Put on the E.T. feed."

We had a dish to pick up the satellite transmission to the East Coast of *Entertainment Tonight*. Due to the time difference, we were seeing the show hours before it would be broadcast locally. The way Washington politicians watched the weekend talkfests, we watched E! and *Entertainment Tonight*. Sometimes we'd picked up interesting tidbits about the competition. More often, we'd get an early heads-up about what the print media would be calling us about the next day. I grabbed the remote out of my desk drawer, and flicked on the set. They had just sent over the promos for tonight's show, and the program itself was about to begin.

"Leading the news tonight is the gala premiere of a new science fiction movie in which Woody Allen plays a well-adjusted person, reports from a plastic surgeon that Dolly Parton has had her whole body lifted, and first, the inside story about that top secret summer release from Graham Studios."

While the show's insipid theme song ran, I dialed Junior's office. I didn't even wait to hear who had picked it up. "Put on *E.T.*," I shouted, and hung up.

"For the past several weeks, moviegoers have been teased mercilessly about the hush-hush megafilm Graham Studios has under wraps for their summer schedule." They showed an abbreviated version of the teaser trailer, then cut to their reporter in the field. She was standing in front of a non-descript building somewhere in the Valley. It was, at the least, nearly a forty-five minute drive from here. What was going on?

"I'm here with Demetri Panakis, of Coates and Panakis, a leading movie supply house which services Graham Studios. Mr. Panakis, what is the nature of your most recent order from Graham?"

Panakis, the swarthy betrayer of Graham Studios and everything it stood for, would be lucky if he didn't find a horse's head in his bed before the day was through. Onscreen, he smiled as if he didn't have a care in the world. After all, what could be wrong? He was on television.

"My company provides costumes and special makeup supplies for several studios. When we got the latest call from Graham, it was our most complicated project yet."

"And what, exactly, did they want?"

"Brogardi clothing and blue latex skull caps."

The scene shifted to the reporter in front of our main gate. "We tried to reach Jake Berman, senior vice president for publicity for Graham Studios, but his office told us he would be out most of the afternoon."

I didn't hear the rest because I was too busy screaming. I had been just about to pick up the message slip that—I saw now—was from this same reporter, and time stamped when I was getting beaten up by Ben in Junior's private health club. I was too late. It was all over, and we hadn't even finished shooting the picture. Damned reporters. Why couldn't they be bought and paid for, like they were in the old days? I raced out of my office, and past Betty's desk. She was answering the phone. I didn't even wait. "Tell him I'm on my way."

Junior's outer office looked like the reception area of a funeral parlor. Word had quickly spread, and most of the people directly responsible to Junior had automatically rushed to his office to get their orders. Would we pull the plug, or tough it out? How important was the element of surprise? Junior's secretary only allowed a few into the inner sanctum. I hoped against hope, but it was useless. Of course I was waved right in.

Junior was at THE DESK. Seated around it were Caroline Sosniak, Dick Lyman, and Gretchen O'Hearn, our chief counsel. Abe was notably absent. I dreaded who would have to tell him there was no film, if that was the decision.

"How the hell did this happen?" thundered Junior. "Don't we have confidentiality agreements with all our suppliers?"

Gretchen pulled out a document from her briefcase. "His partner signed the agreement. Panakis was bound by it, but he was on vacation. Coates apparently never told him."

"Really," said Junior, suddenly dangerously quiet, the calm before the storm. "Well, I hope you find that a comfort when you're on the goddamned unemployment line!"

"Now wait, maybe there's a way we can salvage this," said Caroline, trying to save her chance at film history. "Jake, is there some way we can spin this?"

"I'd like to spin this Greek traitor right back to the Parthenon," shouted Junior. I'd never seen him this steamed before, all red-faced and bulging veins. The usually mild-mannered Junior was turning into an old-time, volcanic studio boss. I was hoping this wasn't going to turn into a 911 call for an ambulance.

Junior's secretary came in quickly, and with her head lowered, hoping that this interruption wouldn't cost her her job. She had a sheaf of papers and, to my horror, she handed them to me. "Just a moment," I muttered to Junior, as I started to read.

"Don't keep it a secret, Jake. If your broker is advising you to sell your stock in our parent company, let us all in on it."

I read the cover note and top sheet, and then I started to laugh. I was afraid I was going to lose it altogether. Dick Lyman reached over and grabbed one of my shoulders. "Get a hold of yourself, man. It can't be as bad as all that."

Dick backed off as I stood up. "Yes, Caroline, there is a way to spin this, and it doesn't involve having the Greco-American Anti-Defamation League picketing the studio." Every eye was on me, including both of Junior's bloodshot ones.

"Did anyone happen to see the entire story?"

They all looked at each other. "I didn't see it at all," said Caroline, "I just got the call to come here immediately."

"Me too," agreed Dick. Gretchen nodded as well.

"Sly?"

Junior had taken his seat. He shook his head almost imperceptibly, and pointed behind us. A large paperweight rested in what was left of his TV screen. "The minute that son of a bitch let the cat out of the bag, I lost control," he said. "So what else did the late Mr. Panakis have to say?"

I smiled. "He revealed that the costumes and head gear were for our new movie, *The Ducklings' Brogardi Adventure*." The note was from Diane, who was about to get a raise and a promotion for keeping her cool after all. While we were running around like headless chickens, she was doing her job. She had had the entire story transcribed, including a summary. Knowing that I would want it immediately, she had risked Junior's wrath by making his secretary bring it in to me.

"*The Duckling's Brogardi Adventure*? What the hell is that?" sputtered Junior.

"Our big, nonexistent summer production that *E.T.* just told the world was our surprise project."

Caroline immediately grasped the implications. "That means we don't have to shut down. They don't know about the movie. Or about Abe."

"That's right. Apparently, Coates and Panakis are our suppliers for all the Duckling movies, so they just naturally assumed the Brogardi costumes were for the next Duckling adventure."

"You mean they were our suppliers," snarled Junior.

"Fine, fire them once we release our movie. In the meantime, if we spin this right, we can keep the press in a frenzy, chasing after their fake movie instead of our real one."

"How are you going to do that?" asked Dick.

"It's simple. Gretchen, we have the whole Duckling cast under long-term contracts, right?"

"We've got 'em for twenty years after they die," she agreed.

"I thought they were just puppets," said Dick.

"Nah," said Junior, suddenly looking like his old self. "Jake's talking about the voice cast."

I acknowledged Junior, and went on. "Now, all we have to do is issue a one-sentence statement denying that there's any Duckling/Brogardi movie, and then refuse all further comment. Then we get the actors to decline all interviews. Gretchen, you were a journalist before you went to law school. What does a reporter do in that situation?"

She grinned. "He or she goes nuts. The denial without explanation is considered a confirmation of the story being denied, and the fact that everyone who would know the details is clamming up is further proof. They can't necessarily publish anything, but they'll pursue it, knowing it has to be true. Except it isn't."

"How do you do that?" asked Caroline, with a hint of admiration. Call it one professional purveyor of fantasy acknowledging another.

"It's your basic P.R. spin: don't lie, tell the truth. It's a much more effective way to spread disinformation. The next Duckling film doesn't even go into production until the fall, and I think they're going to Antarctica or some such place. All we're doing is truthfully denying that there's a Duckling/Brogardi film. But the way we're doing it is going to lead everyone to think we're covering up."

"It's going to cost us," said Greta. "The actors are going to want something to sweeten the deal, if they have to give up several months of public appearances."

"Give them $10,000 apiece, and tell them they'll still have the whole summer, starting Memorial Day weekend. It would be cheap at twice the price," said Junior, sitting back in his chair with a broad grin. "And Dick? Have them send over a new TV for me, will you please? Mine seems to be on the fritz."

I Married a Monster from Outer Space

One of the side effects of the *Entertainment Tonight* story was that I had to be extremely circumspect in getting Radio City Music Hall for our premiere. I arranged it through one of the other divisions of our parent company, promising my counterpart there a block of tickets to the show in exchange for handling the job and not asking any questions.

It turned out to be a lot easier than I had expected. As it happened, the theater had a dark night between the end of their annual Easter pageant and some big music awards show, and if we could guarantee that we'd be in and out in twenty-four hours, they'd be happy to accommodate us. Actually, they were told they were handling a trade show extravaganza for our sister company's unveiling of its new models of supermarket freezers. Why anyone would want the cavernous Music Hall for showcasing industrial merchandise is beyond me, but the theater's booker didn't argue. It was a night that would now be marked in the profit column, rather than as a loss.

That out of the way, my ruse to keep the press off track worked like a charm. The next day we issued a terse statement: "Contrary to a report in the media, Graham Studios has no present plans to make any film involving our beloved Duckling characters and our new friends from Brogard."

The trade papers had a field day attempting to parse that sentence to see what we were really saying, but all inquiries along those lines were met with a friendly but strict "No comment." I didn't want anyone in the press with a relationship with anyone at the studio to get a more detailed denial. The only way this would work is if it appeared that we really did have something to hide. We even got a short feature in *Newsweek*, where their critic speculated as to why we want to keep the project a secret now that our cover was blown.

The one factor we couldn't control was the Brogardi Embassy, but Abe's father—who didn't know what his son was up to—couldn't have been a bigger help if he was on the payroll. "While we welcome visitors to Brogard, and are grateful for the warm welcome the Brogardi have received on Earth, it was the decision of both parties that trade and cultural exchanges would be taken slowly, to avoid too much of a shock to either of our peoples. Therefore, I can categorically deny that there are any plans for Brogardi participation in any of your Hollywood productions."

That last convinced Junior that I was the greatest publicist since P.T. Barnum, and he congratulated me with a magnum of my favorite champagne. The note read simply, "Quack, quack. —Sly." I felt I ought to make the same sort of gesture to Diane, besides moving her up out of reviewing clippings, and sent her and her boyfriend to my favorite restaurant for dinner, arranging that it would be billed to my account. I told the owner—who had bought a boat on the strength of Graham Studio business—that they were to get the best of everything. Evidently, they did. A week later Diane informed me he had proposed.

I responded the only way I could under the circumstances: I told her she'd be fired if they got married before Memorial Day.

Caroline invited me to the rushes one afternoon a few weeks later. After I had saved her film, any real or imagined hostilities between us vanished. She had always been more of a "house director" than an auteur with a strong, individual signature to her films, and she knew that this project was her bid for immortality. Whatever else she accomplished in her career, she would always be the first human to direct a Brogardi actor.

As often happens late in a production, the once well-attended rushes were now playing only to the people who really needed to see them: Caroline, her director of photography, the sound man, and a handful of others. Even Junior, who was taking the producer's credit on the film, didn't bother to show up.

I was there as a guest, but I suspected she wanted a fresh opinion of the footage. I hadn't seen anything except the day I visited Abe on the set, and might catch something everyone else had overlooked. Given the newly tightened security, Junior had to personally approve anyone on the set or in the screening room, and that sort of limited the potential audience.

They were already rolling film when I arrived, so I took a seat a couple of rows back in the small theater, so Caroline could confer privately with her crew. As a reel ended and the screen lit up, she turned and saw me. I waved to let her know I was there, and she waved back. She didn't motion me down. I suspected that, as much as she wanted her privacy with her crew, she might also not want them to hear her conversation with me.

A new reel started, this scene involving Abe, or Yekl, being reconciled with his father. He had become the toast of Broadway, but left his hit show to return to Brogard for the all-important graduation festival for his sister. His father (old-timer William McMurphy done up in Brogardi drag) tells him that he doesn't understand Earth ways or Yekl's life, but as long as he doesn't forsake his Brogardi heritage, he would always be welcomed home.

"Father, you make me so happy," said Abe, with that faraway look he had when he got emotional. Either the scene was really affecting him, or he was turning into the first Brogardi method actor. "We have a lot to learn from Earth."

"And they have a lot to learn from us," countered McMurphy.

"That's very true. And that's why I want to go back, and use my success to introduce our ideas to the Earthans, becoming a goodwill ambassador for Brogard."

"If you do as well as your friend has here, you should bring honor to both worlds." Here the camera pulled back to show that Yekl's manager and platonic friend Melanie (Linda Reid) had entered the room. The shot ended with his mother entering with a traditional Brogardi wine, and the four characters toasting the wonderful friendship between Brogard and Earth.

The scene played a couple more times, as Caroline had printed three takes, and then went to various closeups. There was a problem with McMurphy's closeups.

"Damn it, Al, you said the lighting wasn't going to be a problem." Caroline was angry, and with good reason. In each of the closeups, it was painfully obvious where the line was between the blue headpiece and the makeup.

This went on for several minutes, as they discussed when they could redo the shots, and whether they could do without the closeups altogether. In the end, Caroline opted for the retakes. She was very lucky that Junior was giving her a free hand. The fact that they were working so fast that they were actually a day ahead of schedule might have had something to do with it.

There were some miscellaneous entrances and exits, including one of Abe looking up in what I guessed was Brogardi wonder, although it might have been a stuffy nose, and finally we had seen the day's footage. Caroline conferred with her team a few moments more, and then they left, either to perform their assigned tasks or to go home and try to get some rest. With another two weeks of production to go, nerves were undoubtedly on edge.

At last it was just Caroline and me. "So," she said, getting directly to the point, "What do you think?"

"I think you're a little shaky on character development."

She looked at me askance, as if I she was now sorry she had invited me, and then realized I was making a joke. "Okay, wise guy, what did you think of the footage you saw?"

"Other than McMurphy's hairline, it looked damned good. The story is pure schmaltz, but we knew that going in. I'm real impressed with the job you're doing with Abe."

She shook her head. "I'll be happy to take the credit at the Oscars next year, but I'm simply guiding him. Jake, our boy is a natural. He's a born actor."

"Well, you know, this may be hitting a little close to home for him. He's not exactly on the best of terms with his real father."

"He's told me. I told him to use those feelings for his character, and his eyes lit up. 'What a marvelous idea,' he said, the way he does whenever something new excites him."

"Are you sure his eyes lit up? Some of his expressions can be pretty baffling until you get used to them," I said. "What was that business where it looks like he's suffering from an ingrown toenail?"

She laughed. "It's a closeup that we're going to intercut with documentary footage we're trying to obtain of Brogard. His character is supposed to be overwhelmed by conflicting emotions when he returns home after his triumph on Earth."

"Well, they might get it on Brogard, but I don't know if it's going to play in Peoria without subtitles."

Now I saw why Junior had wanted Caroline for the job. Instead of taking the criticism personally, she instantly set about seeing if it could be fixed. "Hmm, I suppose I could have Abe loop a line or two over the Brogardi footage. Yeah, that will work," she told herself. "Thanks, Jake."

"Where's Abe now? I thought I'd drop in and tell him how the early reviews are going."

"Don't you dare spook him with any criticism," she said, suddenly firm. "Any notes to my actors go through me."

"Yes, ma'am!" I said, smartly saluting. "Is it okay to talk about the weather?"

"Sorry, Jake," she said, laughing. "I've been putting in sixteen-hour days for the last month. Abe went back to his bungalow. His call for tomorrow isn't until noon, now that we have to reshoot McCarthy's closeups. He'd probably appreciate the company."

"Great. I'll give him the good news."

I knocked on the bungalow door, but there was no answer. Finding it unlocked, I went in, figuring Abe would be right back. He wasn't supposed to leave the lot during the production, so he couldn't have gone very far. The living room was a lot neater than it had been the last time I was here. I couldn't put my finger on it, and then I realized the difference: he had put all his videos away. Either the clutter had been getting to him, or Lyman had arranged for housekeeping for Abe.

I sat on the couch, grabbing one of the trades off the coffee table, looking to while away a few minutes, when I heard the voices from the bedroom.

"Lower... lower... yes, that's it, oh, that's perfect... Right there!"

"Abe? Who's there?" I called out. I pulled out my cell phone, ready to call studio security if this was a break-in. I peered into the bedroom, and got the surprise of my life. There was Abe, getting a back rub from a very naked Linda Reid. We all screamed at once.

Abe finally managed to blurt out an intelligible question, "Jake, what are you doing here?"

I backed out of the room quickly. Part of my mind was fixing the image of Linda Reid for permanent storage, while the rest of it was realizing that we were in deep, deep trouble. Abe came running out after me, tying the cord around his bathrobe as he did so.

"I can't believe you just walked in, Jake," said Abe, sounding disappointed. "I had been told you Earthans believed a man's home is his castle."

I looked at him, not quite believing what I was hearing. Then I exploded. "Are you out of your mind? What the hell are you doing in there?"

Abe turned slightly purple, but then brightened. "I told you Earth gravity tired me out, didn't I? I'm sure I did. Linda and I were—"

"I don't want to hear about it," I shouted, cutting him off, "Don't you realize what would happen if this got out? Don't you know what this would do to the film?"

"No, Jake, I don't," he replied, sounding puzzled. "What's the problem?"

"What's the problem? What's the problem? Haven't all those shlocky sci-fi films taught you anything? Don't you know that if there's one thing humans don't like it's *aliens from space fucking our women*?" I sat down on the couch with a thud. "Why me? Every time I solve one problem on this film, another one takes its place." I looked to Abe for a response, but he was gone.

He came hurrying back with, of all things, his guidebook. "Now hold on, let me do this myself," he said, flipping through the pages. He finally found what he was looking for, and read the entry. Then he looked at me disapprovingly.

"According to this, that's a word one doesn't use in polite company, or in front of children." I was stunned into momentarily silence. "Do you speak to Susan like that?" he continued.

I leapt to my feet. "Abe, this isn't about me, this is about you. All right," I said, catching my breath, "there's no need to panic yet. No one else knows about this. We've just got to stop it right now."

"What are you going to do? Ground him?" Linda had pulled on a T-shirt and jeans, and come out to join the fray. We both looked at Abe, who was looking nervously around at the floor.

"Abe?"

"I was looking for the loose electrical wires. I certainly don't want to get a shock. I've had a healthy respect for electrical power since the time my school took us to a generating plant…"

"It's just an expression, babe," said Linda. "It means that Jake here thinks he can order you around like he's your father, and not let you go out on dates."

"This is not happening," I announced, "I cannot believe I found Abe in bed with some starlet, and we're discussing American slang."

Linda cut me with an icy stare. "Starlet?! I'll have you know that I spent three years on the road with the national company of *Cats*."

"Really?" said Abe, "Then maybe you can answer a question that's been bothering me—"

"All right," I said, cutting him off. "It's up to me to be the grown-up. Abe, remember when I told you about my father-in-law and how some people are bigots?"

"Of course."

"Well, he's not the only one. Unfortunately, there's a lot of them. And some of them buy tickets to our movies. Now, one of the things we want to do with this movie is cement the friendship between our two worlds. Surely you see that?"

"Oh yes, that's been discussed from the beginning."

"Now Abe… friend… do you understand that some people may not be inclined to go to our movie if they think the star is intent on having his way with human women because he can't keep his blue dick in his pants?"

"Actually," said Linda, "It's more of a—"

"I don't want to know. We are not having this conversation. You," I said directly to Linda, "are leaving. Immediately."

"I don't think you'll find any language in my contract that gives you the right to govern my private life, Jake."

Abe put his hand on her shoulder. "Now just a second, dear, Jake may have a point. Certainly they have reason to want to keep the focus on the movie rather than my personal life, for at least a little while."

"Now you're talking sense, Abe," I said, encouraging him. He turned to me. "How long are we talking about? A few weeks? A couple of months?"

"Three years."

"Three years!" shouted Linda. "Just how did you come up with that figure?"

"Well, the premiere is set for early May, we go wide Memorial Day, the home video will be out at Christmas, the cable window will be next winter. Then there's overseas sales, and the TV deals—broadcast and syndicated, and we have an option on a sequel—"

"If you think I'm going to plan my social life around your business plans—"

"Linda, I think we need to talk," said Abe. "Jake, could you give us a moment?"

"Sure." I slipped out, and waited outside. I figured that Abe would now explain to Linda that they had made a mistake, that too much was at stake to risk for fleeting moments of pleasure, and that a scandal would reflect badly not only on the film, but on Earth/Brogard relations as well. About five minutes later, Linda left, gliding frostily past me on her way to her car. She took off without looking back.

I knocked on Abe's door, and he let me in, handing me a small glass filled with a chocolatey sweet drink. "It's a Brandy Alexander. Linda got me a bartender's book so that I could experiment with—"

"I think you've done more than enough experimenting for one day," I said, putting down the drink. "Abe, what could you have been thinking? Even if we put the potential for bad publicity aside, there are other questions, like what about disease?"

"Are you suggesting that Linda is unclean?" he said, not looking at all pleased. Whether it was at her potential impurity or my insensitive remark, I couldn't be certain.

"No, no. I meant that you and she are literally from two different worlds. What if she gave you something, or you gave it to her, for which the other one had no built-in immunity?"

Abe broke out into a hearty wheeze. "You mean like in *The War of the Worlds*, where the Martians all keel over from a rhinovirus?"

"Well, not exactly. But you get the general idea."

"Jake, you really haven't been paying attention. The medical experts on both worlds said they were startled by just how similar our makeups were, and how there was no risk of infection. Why do you suppose we're allowed to wander all over your world, and Earthans are all over ours? This was big, big news about six months ago. The doctors said it would completely rewrite the biological sciences."

"Guess I missed it," I said, kicking myself mentally. "But what about pregnancy? I do recall reading that they have no idea if our two species can produced offspring, and the potential uproar over the possibility was so great on both planets that all research was put on the back burner."

Abe came over and put his arm around me. "I'm not quite clear how this works on Earth, but we have means of preventing unwanted pregnancies on Brogard. Linda said that… wait, what did she call it?… Oh, my 'protection' was far more effective…"

I stepped away. "Abe, I do not want to know this. I have never wanted to know the intimate details of the sex lives of my friends, regardless of what planet they were born on."

"There's no need to be squeamish—"

"Yes, there is. There is because there are an awful lot of moviegoers who will take an instant disliking to you if the first thing they hear about you is not that you're an important new acting talent, but that you're bedding down your human costar."

Abe startled. "Important new acting talent?"

"Yes, that was the reason I came over. I just saw some of the rushes, and you were great. Caroline called you a natural. You could have a great future in the movies. I would just hate to see it cut off before it even started."

"Is that like Elizabeth's great-grandson becoming president?"

"Huh?"

"Never mind. If I don't see Linda, though, I'm still going to need my massages. I don't understand why you're not exhausted in this gravity all the time."

"Well, that's easy enough. Ben was asking for you over at the health club. He can do whatever Linda was doing."

Abe thought this over. "So you're saying it's okay to have sex with Ben, but not with Linda?"

"What?! Don't even go there…" I caught him trying to hide his laughter, but I could hear him wheezing. "You're getting to be a bit too good of an actor, if you ask me. Now, Abe, I want you to promise me that you'll stop seeing Linda."

He looked me square in the eyes. "Jake, I promise that the only place anyone will see my blue skin next to hers is on screen."

We shook hands on it.

The Horror of Party Beach

The film's production was mercifully coming to an end at last. There would still be a tremendous amount of work to do in post-production, and I would have my hands full supervising a publicity campaign that could only begin after we had the premiere. Usually, we'd have a lot of advance publicity building up to the opening, so that moviegoers would be well aware of our project by the time it was finally playing at the local googolplex. But although we would soon pass—if we hadn't already—the date anyone could rush a low-budget ripoff into the theaters ahead of us, Junior felt we had to play out the surprise angle to the end. If the press was filled with speculation about how good an actor Abe was, the mystery would be lost by the time people could actually see for themselves.

Caroline was pressing for test screenings, so she could get some feedback in tweaking the film, but Junior flat-out refused. "There's no such thing as a secret screening anymore," he told her. "Five minutes after the houselights come up, a dozen reviews are floating around the internet." He was right, but it meant that security, as well as keeping Abe out of the spotlight, would continue to be a major concern. I hadn't mentioned my finding him *in flagrante delicto* with Linda, but clearly making sure Abe didn't make any headlines prior to the premiere would be a priority.

Today, however, was the final day of shooting, and it was a time for celebration. Most of the cast and crew would be departing, and traditionally they had a big farewell party after the last shot was in the can. And why not? Not only had this been an intense project to shoot, but every one of them was a potential security risk. They had all signed secrecy agreements, of course, but all you needed was one disgruntled ex-employee to blow the whole thing. This was our way of keeping the positive feelings going. After the New York opening, they'd all be invited back for a private screening and another party before the film opened in L.A.

Ironically, the last shot of the movie was the scene where Yekl is auditioning for his first serious acting role, which takes place fairly early in the story. Most people don't realize that a film isn't shot in chronological order, but is based on the availability of actors and sets.

Since all that was needed was a bare stage for this scene, it had been held in reserve as a substitute in the shooting schedule, in case whatever was planned for that day suddenly got tied up for one reason or another.

Junior was already on the set, and I had invited Larissa and Susie to join us. Visitors were usually frowned upon, especially on this film, but since Abe had been a guest in our home, no one raised any objection. Betty, Diane, and the rest of my team were there as well. This was a special project, for which they had performed above and beyond the call of duty, and they were as entitled to party as anyone else. For many, it was the first time they had been included in such festivities, and some of them acted like kids making their first trip to Disneyland.

"Pretty exciting, eh Betty?"

She smiled. "It certainly is, Mr. Berman. But it was much more exciting to watch them film the opening night scene, where Abe suddenly realizes he's going to be a big success."

I looked at her. "When did you see that?"

"When they shot it, two weeks ago. Abe invited me down to the set. He wanted to exchange vacation tips during lunch time, and he invited me to stick around for the shooting." Serves me right for taking long lunch hours myself. I hadn't even noticed she was missing.

On the set, which was dressed as a bare theater stage, Abe was pacing and muttering to himself. Susie tugged at my sleeve.

"Can I go say hello to Abe, Daddy?"

"No, dear, he's busy rehearsing now. You'll have plenty of time to see him afterward."

She went back to Larissa, looking for something to keep her occupied in the meantime. Finally, an assistant director shouted, "Quiet on the set, everyone! This is going to be a take!"

Caroline exchanged a final few words with Abe, then returned to her seat. "And, action!"

In character, Abe addressed an unseen audience, "I know you don't get many Brogardi trying out, sir, but if you'll just give me a chance..."

"Cut!"

They did it another time, and then Abe left the stage. If I recalled the script correctly, they would then cut to the director who is auditioning him, who tells him to do his Shakespearean monologue. Ordinarily in a scene like this, you'd get a few lines everyone was familiar with, like Hamlet's soliloquy or Marc Antony's funeral oration for Caesar. If the script was trying to score points and be ironic, especially with Abe in the part, they might have him deliver Shylock's plea for tolerance. ("Hath not a Jew eyes?… If you prick us do we not bleed?") Instead, incredibly, the script had Yekl doing the opening of *Richard III*.

"Quiet everyone!"

"And, action!"

Abe came out in what was either his or Caroline's imagined interpretation of how a struggling Brogardi actor would play the villainous hunchback king, who was more a creation of Shakespeare than of history. Abe had pulled off his sports jacket and wrapped it around his shoulders, one of which was raised slightly.

"Now is the winter of our discontent, made glorious summer by this son of York," he rasped, loping about the stage. Though he delivered the whole monologue, it would be intercut with reaction shots from the director and producer, who were bowled over by his supposedly masterful portrayal. In typical Hollywood fashion, those reaction shots had been filmed a month ago. One line struck me as unintentionally funny, and I had to bring my hand to my mouth to stifle a laugh.

"And therefore, since I cannot prove a lover, to entertain these fair well-spoken days," Abe said, "I am determined to prove a villain, and hate the idle pleasures of these days." Abe was no villain, but it was only because of my quick thinking that he wasn't going to be able to prove himself as a lover either, at least not here on Earth.

I noticed that Caroline was filming the scene with two cameras, one stationary and one handheld. She really wanted to get this the first time out. If Shakespeare is hard for American actors I could only imagine what it was like for someone from another world. Abe had finished, and stood still, his head bent. Then, reaching up for his jacket, which ended up over his arm, he stood tall, trying to gauge the reaction from weeks ago.

"And, cut!"

The sound stage filled with applause. Abe, who had apparently become something of a ham, waved to the crowd and took his bows. Caroline conferred with her d.p. and sound man, and they both nodded. She walked to the stage and put her arm around Abe.

"Ladies and gentlemen, that's a wrap!" She turned and gave him a big hug, as people started packing up equipment, or at least moving it out of the way for the party. Those without any immediate official functions headed for the buffet and bar, which had been set up on the far end. Well, almost everyone.

"Abe! Abe! Abe!" I heard the high-pitched squeal before I saw the diminutive form racing across the sound stage, dodging grips and technicians, and rushing up to the raised platform.

"Susan, what are you doing here? Did you get to see me act?" He reached down over the lip of the stage, itself only about six inches above the floor, and lifted her up. "I'm so glad to see you."

"I brought you a picture," she said, handing him a folded-up piece of construction paper. He put her down and began to unfold it, while Larissa and I hurried across the room to prevent Susie from getting into any more trouble.

On the paper was a crayon drawing of a blue stick figure with a very round head holding what looked like a banana.

"This is very interesting, Susan. Is this supposed to be me?"

"Of course it is," she said, as if there could be no questioning of this obvious likeness.

"Hi, Abe," said Larissa, "You were quite good." She looked at the picture. "Susan, why is Abe holding a banana?"

"It's not a banana, Mommy. It's an Oscar. It's a picture of Abe winning the Oscar for having the best movie."

"I think that's the one I get to collect," said a voice behind us. It was Junior, with a waitress in tow with a bottle of champagne and several glasses. He had a paper cup which he handed to Susan, explaining, "When Abe gets to win, it will be for being the best actor."

When we all had champagne—except for Susie, whose cup was filled with ginger ale—the assistant director shouted, "Quiet on the set, everyone!"

The room hushed, as Junior raised his glass. "I want to thank all of you for being a part of history. I believed that if we all worked together, we could make a movie that would commemorate the friendship of Earth and Brogard, and present audiences with their first Brogardi movie star. You're all in on the secret now, but in a little over two months time, the whole world—two whole worlds—will know. To Abe!"

The room thundered in response as we all drank to Abe. He had a funny expression on his face, one I wasn't familiar with, but then it passed. He leaned over to Susie to clink glasses. "And to my best friends on Earth," he said quietly, rising and clinking with Larissa and myself as well.

"It's five P.M.," said Junior to the crowd, "You're all on your own time now. Let's party!"

A band struck up some music, and the celebration was under way.

Susie was petering out. Since we had two cars here, Larissa headed out with her. This was no mere social function for me, and she knew I had to stay for a while longer.

"Kiss the baby for me," I said.

"Going so soon?" said Abe, joining us.

"Can't be helped. Your secret friend is very, very tired," Larissa said, smiling. Susie stifled a yawn, and gave Abe a hug.

"You're going to come visit us soon, right?" she asked.

"Don't you worry. I'm sure we'll be getting together real soon."

It turned out to be sooner than any of us thought. Not twenty minutes later, I found myself cornered by Junior. "Jake, we've got a problem."

"No, we've just resolved a problem. The shoot is over. It's all editing and planning the premiere now. Our biggest problem is over."

"No, it turns out we're going to need Abe for a lot of the post-production work."

Typically the actors, if needed, come back for a day of "looping." That involves re-recording dialogue to match what was filmed where there was a problem with the soundtrack. Clearly, Junior had more in mind.

"What gives?"

"The sound department tells us that he's got to do his own Foley work."

This was unheard of. The Foley artists were people who dubbed in things like footsteps and other natural sounds that weren't picked up during the recording of the dialogue. No one does their own Foley work. Look at the credits of any feature film.

"This is a joke, right?"

"Remember all that stuff about Earth's gravity being slightly stronger?"

"So?"

"Turns out it affects the way they walk, at least on Earth. They showed me a test reel with human footsteps dubbed in. It sounded as phony as a three-dollar bill."

"What does a three-dollar bill sound like?" I asked, to Junior's stony silence. "C'mon, no one can tell the difference."

"Jake, trust me on this. If I can tell the difference, other people will notice. Remember, we're hoping this film will be our opening wedge in cracking the Brogardi market. It's got to be real, and it's got to sound real."

"And that's why we had Marj Grange and Bill McMurphy playing his parents?"

"You know why we had to do that. Abe is our ticket to authenticity. And that's why we need him to do the music, too."

At this point, I was wondering why they didn't just have him edit the film as well. It turned out that they wanted Abe to play some traditional melodies for a few scenes, and if we hired other Brogardi musicians, it would exponentially increase the security risk.

"What makes you think Abe can play an instrument?"

Junior smiled. "Didn't you know? It was his major. He's even selected some of the music. He said he studied it in school. Really weird sounding stuff. Abe said it only had five notes, in different combinations."

I tried to look at the bright side, but I sensed what was coming. "If you ever let me actually promote this movie, this is going to be a publicist's dream. In the meantime, does that mean Abe has to remain on the lot?"

Junior smiled again. He was making me nervous. He seemed to be enjoying this far too much. "No. As a matter of fact, we're not going to need him for a couple of weeks while they're assembling the first rough cut. At that point, they'll know where he's needed in post."

"So you're sending him back to Dad?"

"As it turns out, his father is back on Brogard for consultations with his government. So I thought it would be better if Abe stayed with you."

"Well, I've come to really enjoy my time with Abe, Sly, and you saw how my family adores him, but I don't know if we can put him up for several weeks. Besides, someone's bound to spot him coming or going, and you really can't expect him to just sit in the basement."

"I agree one hundred percent," said Junior, "That's why, as of this moment, you're on vacation. At double pay."

"But… but…"

"No need to thank me."

Thank him? I wanted to kill him. I had the premiere to plan, the massive press and publicity campaign that had to be ready to begin immediately thereafter, not to mention all our other releases, which I had been neglecting.

"And don't worry about your work," he continued, "Most of it has been reassigned, and the stuff relating to *The Brogardi* has all been labeled 'Rush' and 'Not to go out without Jake's approval.' You won't have to do anything but approve or disapprove when you get back."

"But…"

"Happy holidays, Jake. You're doing a hell of a job."

I think I lost an hour or two of the party after that. It was after nine, as it started to wind down, that I spotted Abe near the bar, drinking something with an umbrella in it and talking to… Linda Reid. I tried to be nonchalant as I walked over to them, but Linda spotted me before I was halfway there, pecked him on the cheek, and took off.

"Guess I won't be getting her vote for most popular guy on the lot," I said.

"Slow comfortable screw?" asked Abe.

I thought I was hearing things. "Pardon?"

"My drink. It's a mixture of orange juice, vodka, sloe gin, and Southern Comfort. I knew you Earthans were ahead of us in anesthesiology, but I really had no idea. I'm feeling no pain tonight."

"Don't overdo it, or you'll be feeling plenty of pain in the morning." Abe not only swam like a fish; it was beginning to look like he drank like one, too. "So, what did Linda have to say, besides good-bye?"

"Well, it really wasn't good-bye. She starts work on a made-for-cable film on Monday right here in L.A. She said Hollywood's a small town, so we might run into each other again real soon."

"I'm afraid that's not possible, Abe."

"I appreciate your concern, but the filming is over, and I should be able to run my life as I see fit."

Uh oh, this meant trouble. "We've been over this, Abe, and I don't think you necessarily realize what's in your own best interests," I told him firmly. We had become good friends, but business was business. "We made an agreement, and you've got to stick to it."

Abe looked at me funny for a moment. "You know, it's uncanny. If I close my eyes, you sound just like my father." I decided not to pursue that line of discussion. It couldn't do either of us any good.

"Junior tells me that you've got to come back in a few weeks and have a lot to do in finishing the film."

"Well, you don't expect me to just be a prisoner in my bungalow until then, do you?"

"Of course not. Junior just put me on vacation, too. We're all going to get out of town for a while."

"Your whole family?"

"No, just you, me, and Larissa." That is, unless Larissa decided to kill me.

"Where are we going?"

Where were we going? Good question. It had to be some place where Abe wouldn't stick out like a sore thumb, because there were a lot of Brogardi around, and where I wouldn't be noticed as a studio exec by other people in the industry or the press. There was one only place on Earth at that moment in time that filled that bill, and like it or not, we were going there.

"We're going to the Catskills."

Destination Moon

We couldn't just take Susie out of school, and it wouldn't be much of a vacation for Larissa if she had to take care of Elizabeth while I was partying with Abe, so we got her parents to come in for a week and look after the kids. Larissa had to be back in court the second week, so she'd return home, and my parents would visit and help out with the kids. There was going be one point when Larissa, my parents, and her parents were all there at the same time, and I was glad I would missing the changing of the guard. My parents adored Larissa, but my father and Sidney represented two of the last factions that had not come to terms following the arrival of the Brogardi.

"You have nothing to worry about," said Claire, as the car came to pick us up for the airport. I always worry when someone says that, but there wasn't anything I could do about it. "We're going to have a great time, aren't we Susan?"

"Why can't I go with you?" she whined, ignoring her grandmother. She was a delightful child, but when the whining started, she became the irresistible force meeting the immovable object. Something had to give, and it wouldn't be pleasant. "How come *you* get to go have a good time with Abe, and I don't?"

"But Susan, this is still part of the secret plan," said Abe in his gentlest voice. "When we get back, I'll see if you can come over and see how I have to run in place for the microphones, and then I'll show you how to play the [something incomprehensible here] just like my mother did. I bet you never played the [whatever], have you?"

"Play it? I'll give you a hundred bucks if she can even pronounce it," I said.

"Mommy," said one of my future heirs, ignoring me, "Will I be able to play with Abe when he comes back?"

Larissa looked at Abe, and then me, and then Susie. "I don't see why not. But now I want you to be a help for your Grandma and Grandpa, and show them where everything is."

The storm had passed. "Come on, Grandma, let me show you where Mr. Bunny likes to hide." There were another round of quick good-byes, then we loaded up the car and headed to the airport.

Of course, one doesn't just fly from Los Angeles to the Catskills, even if it was now the location of the world's first spaceport. In order to provide clearance for both Earth and Brogardi vessels, the entirety of Sullivan County was declared a "no fly zone" to regular aircraft. Thus, we had to fly to New York City, and then find ground transportation for the two-hour trip up to the mountains. I understood why the Brogardi had selected this out-of-the-way place for their first landing, but now it just seemed inconvenient. I think that continued to be a part of their reasoning, so that the port would not become a three-ring circus.

Of course, that seriously underestimated human ingenuity and the hunger of a region that had been starved to a near-shadow of its former robust self. With the establishment of the port on the former golf course, the hotels were back in business. Indeed, new ones were opening up, a conference center was under construction, and those who had business with the Brogardi—or had hopes of obtaining such—found it prudent to have their own base of operations there.

The resort hotels continued to do well as resorts, since it was also an easy way for humans and Brogardi to mingle socially, satisfying the natural curiosity of both groups. That's why Betty had booked us into the Raleigh Hotel in South Fallsburgh, a five-minute drive from the Concord Spaceport.

The Thompsonville Road exit off of Route 17 took us through a long stretch of the backwoods, broken up only by signs letting us know that ground would soon be broken for a new shopping mall, office complex, or yet another resort hotel. It probably would have been more efficient to just build high rise hotels, but since most of the recreation and entertainment in this remote area was located at the resorts, the traditional model remained the norm.

We passed one weather-beaten sign that promised, "Casinos Mean Jobs," dating back to a failed attempt to introduce gambling into the region as a means to revive it. Somebody had crossed out the word "Casinos" and replaced it with "Brogard." If there were still areas where people liked our friends from space, so long as they didn't move in next door, the Catskills wasn't one of them. Hiding out here with Abe was looking like it was an inspired idea.

We pulled into the Raleigh Hotel driveway, and were stopped at the gate for photographs and fingerprints, the heightened sense of security being part of the downside of the new boom times. Once we were cleared, we were driven up to the hotel, where the driver and the bell captain would negotiate the fate of our luggage.

"Sure is busy," I said to the driver, as I gave him his tip.

"Nah, this is nothing. Tomorrow's the big check-in day."

The first order of business was to get checked in, so I left Larissa and Abe with the bags as I headed to the registration desk. The driver was right. Things were bustling at the moment, but I was able to walk right up to the desk, where a young woman whose nametag identified her as "Bonnie" was on the telephone. She put up a finger to me, indicating she had seen me, and would tend to my needs in just a moment.

"No, Liza, you can't shampoo the dog in the bathtub... I don't care what they did on TV, the dog won't like it... Well, when you're a mother, you can let your kids do whatever they want... I have to go now. Leave the dog alone." She hung up the phone, and turned to me with a quickly placed-on smile. "Kids, they're always up to something."

"I have two myself," I agreed, hoping this wasn't going to turn into a parental stress support group. "The name is Berman. I have two rooms reserved."

She tapped in the name on her keypad, and nodded with satisfaction at her screen. "Yes, you have two adjoining rooms in the Kennedy wing. One is for you and Mrs. Berman, and the other is..." she turned to the screen, "...for a Mr. Gezunt." She looked up in surprise. "Not *the* Gezunt?"

"No, no," I hurriedly replied, "I'm told it's a very common name there."

She nodded, and tapped some more keys. "If I can just have your credit card?"

I slid the plastic across the counter. It came back with the keys, a receipt, and a tip card. That was another quaint Catskills custom that hadn't died out: everyone you met there had their hand out. The tipping got so complex that they gave you a card with the "suggested" per diem amounts.

I quickly scanned down the list to see if Bonnie was entitled to any of my money.

"No, don't bother," she interrupted, "I don't get tipped."

"Thanks," I said, walking back across the cavernous lobby looking for Larissa, Abe, and the baggage.

Behind me, under her breath, I could've sworn Bonnie added, "Damn it."

Our rooms were on the E floor of the Kennedy Wing, the newest and most modern part of the hotel, although the whole place had been heavily refurbished in the last few months, and renovations seemed to be ongoing in what the sign assured us was the "Sammy Davis, Jr. Wing." Apparently, the long-dead entertainer had once had some connection to the hotel. I wonder if his family knew he was memorialized in such a fashion.

For that matter, what did President John F. Kennedy—who as far as I knew had never set foot in the place—have to do with the hotel? As we followed the bellman and luggage cart down the hallway overlooking the indoor pool, there was a portrait of the 35th President hanging near the elevators. Given the pattern, I was wondering if, perhaps, the other areas of the hotel weren't named for other people connected with the legendary Hollywood "Rat Pack." Perhaps the nightclub was named for Frank Sinatra, or the bar for Dean Martin.

The bellman unlocked our door, and said he'd be right back with our luggage, moving down the hall to let Abe into his room. The room was light and airy, with two double beds. I wasn't sure if the implication was that Larissa and I each needed our own bed, or that we would be holding an orgy in our room. I glanced down at the tip card, which informed me that I'd be ransoming back our luggage at a dollar a bag. Since Larissa can't even travel overnight without six bags, and we'd be repeating the process at checkout, I was glad this was all being billed back to the studio. Double vacation pay or not, this was on Junior's tab. Finally, we were settled. I opened the door that connected us to Abe's room, and knocked on his closed door on the other side. He opened it up and looked at me in surprise. It took him a moment to make the connection, and then he gave a little wheeze. "Very clever," he said. "I suppose it cuts down on wear and tear of the hallway carpet."

"I'm sure that was their first concern," I said.

I wanted to get organized, but Larissa wanted to take a shower, while Abe decided he needed a nap. After I finished unpacking my one suitcase,

I went out to make our arrangements in the dining room, the nightclub, and the health club. Everyone assured me that we would get excellent seating or—at the health club—timing, especially after they found their pockets a little heavier and mine a little lighter. At this rate, I was going to need to get to an ATM before the week was out. I had been planning to put everything on my gold card, which usually included the tips as well.

On the way back from the nightclub, I stopped in at the sundry shop to check out the souvenirs. There were T-shirts that said, "My parents went to Earth and all I got was this lousy T-shirt," and buttons that read, "Kiss me, I'm Brogardi." I asked the bored woman behind the counter if this stuff sold.

"Oh, yes, but reaction's mixed. Some tut-tut, and then buy a sweatshirt with just the Raleigh logo on it, while others buy several of each item. I guess only some of them have a sense of humor," she suggested.

Indeed. The lucky ones with the sense of humor knew better than to buy this crap. Then I heard some wheezing behind me, and saw two youngish looking Brogardi examining a poster that was entitled, "Ten reasons the Brogardi landed at the Concord." Item number six was, "They were bringing back Elvis."

"We'll take a half a dozen of them," said one. "Could you wrap them up?"

I was crossing the lobby when I saw Abe coming from the other direction.

"Jake, there you are. Larissa said she'd be at least an hour, and suggested I take a walk around the hotel." Oh, she did, did she? I could see I'd be having a little chat with her as to the purpose of this trip. It was not about giving Abe new opportunities to get into trouble.

We happened to be standing right in front of the lobby bar, and since it was a good two hours until dinner—giving us both plenty of time to wash up and change—I suggested a drink. It was not named for Dean Martin, I noticed, but it was designed as a miniature nightclub, serving the function of providing liquor and music when the actual nightclub wasn't open. No one was performing at the moment, and most of the patrons were sitting around the bar or in the lobby area itself. On one side of the bar were stools, since one had to step down into the club area, but Abe grabbed one of the lower lounge seats on the lobby side. As I took the seat next to him, the bartender came over to ask, "What'll you have?"

"Jack Daniels and soda," I said.

"A Cossack Charge," said Abe.

We both looked at him.

"It's a drink."

"Describe it," demanded the bartender.

"It's vodka, cognac, and cherry brandy, but I'm not sure about the proportions," he said.

The guy turned back to the cash register, and pulled out a book to the side of it. He started flipping through it. "Well, I'll be damned. Here it is. You got it, mister," he said, grabbing the appropriate bottles.

I looked at the bartender, and then at Abe in disbelief. "Are you really planning on going through the bartender's guide, trying every last drink?"

"No," replied Abe, as the Cossack's Charge was set before him, "Only the ones that sound interesting." He took a sip. "How is it?" the bartender asked. We both looked.

"Interesting," said Abe.

At precisely 7 P.M., the doors to the dining room opened, and the crush of people in the lobby began pouring through the twin entrances. Those who had not yet bothered to find out where they were seated now had to stand in line at the *maître d*'s station, but Larissa, Abe, and I breezed right through. We were seated in the far corner, near the windows, and on the opposite end from the kitchen. I'd be able to tell soon enough—from the heat or lack thereof of our entrees—whether this was a good table. Part of the supposed charm of Catskills dining was that it was like being on a cruise ship: you were presented with companions who would share your meals with you. Our problem was that our threesome didn't fit into any neat category. They couldn't exactly seat us with another "Earth couple and single Brogardi male."

Already at the table were a trio of academics who were there for some scientific conference. We exchanged pleasantries, and then they were lost in their arcana, coming up for air only when the waiter or busboy was taking orders for the next course. The other two seats were soon filled by a young Brogardi couple who, amazingly, were newlyweds.

They, too, only had eyes for each other—or at least as far as we could tell. They only seemed to show up for dinner.

The first course was cantaloupe, and the entire room was a sea of orange wedges, as the places had already been set. Our waiter came over to introduce himself as Zvi, an Israeli medical student taking a year off to earn money for school, and to remind us that he needed tipping. Of course he wasn't that blatant. He just reminded us of the Catskills joke that one should always be nice to one's waiter, because you might be looking up at him from an operating table someday. Point made.

"So, which soup would you like this evening? We have matzo ball soup, consomme with egg flakes, or bouillon en tasse."

He took each of our orders until he got to Abe. Abe was having trouble with the menu. "What's the difference between the three soups?"

Zvi leaned over conspiratorially. "Confidentially, there's no difference. They have one big pot of chicken soup in the back, and three sets of cups: one with matzo ball, one with egg flakes, and one that's empty. That's the en tasse. If you'd like some extra en tasse, I'll use my pull in the kitchen for you."

This was obviously shtick he had done many times before, and he waited for the appreciative chuckles, which he got. Except from Abe. "It's all chicken soup?" he asked with some disappointment. "I think I'll skip the soup course."

"Don't worry, Abe," said Larissa, "I'm sure they'll have something else tomorrow."

"Absolutely," agreed Zvi. "Tomorrow the chef told me he's making his specialty for lunch."

"Yes?"

"Cream of broccoli."

Fortunately, Abe was able to find an entree that he wanted: flanken. It's boiled beef on a bone, served with horseradish, and is apparently a holdover from the Catskills' old days as a Jewish vacation spot. Zvi told us that, in the five years he had worked at the hotel while attending school in the States, Abe was the first person who had ever ordered the flanken. After asking Abe if he would mind, Larissa and I had the soup and some roast chicken.

It was delicious.

*   *   *

Normally after a meal like that, all I'd want to do is watch some TV or read a book, and then go to bed. But at a resort, the fun is just beginning. After dinner, we went back to our rooms at one end of the hotel to freshen up, then crossed the lobby, passing the dining room where the last stragglers were finally leaving, and headed to the nightclub, at the other end of the hotel. My baksheesh to the nightclub *maître d'*—a totally different person from the dining room *maître d'*—had gotten us a table near the stage, but off to the side. It was like I had paid enough not to be ignored, but not enough to be noticed. As it turned it out, that was exactly the right thing.

But first we had to be seated, and our drink orders taken. Larissa ordered a white wine, while I stuck with the Jack Daniels from earlier in the day. The cocktail waitress, a twenty-something in a tasteful but somewhat tight and somewhat short outfit, asked Abe what he would like.

"I'd like to get between the sheets," he said.

This time, it was Larissa who reacted. "Abe, you can't just say that!"

"Why not? It's what I want."

The waitress looked at him, wondering whether she should speak her mind or try to salvage her tip. "Look, mister, we're not allowed to do that with the customers."

"Why? Are you out of rum?"

"Is this is another drink, Abe?" I could see this was going to be a very long vacation.

The waitress said she would check and be right back. Five minutes later she returned, all smiles. "One wine, one Jack Daniels, and one Between the Sheets. The bartender said it's with his compliments. No one's asked him to make that one in years."

Between the Sheets turns out to be a concoction involving rum, Cointreau, lemon juice, and brandy. I was going to have find out where Abe had packed his bartender's guide and take it away from him. There were some things Brogardi man was not meant to know, especially if it involved a cocktail shaker. Within a few days, Abe was a favorite at every bar in the hotel. There was one guy in his sixties who would spot us crossing the lobby and shout with his latest offering, "Hey, Abe. How about a Soul Kiss?"

The mind boggled. But Abe just waved back. "Maybe later. I'm off for a massage."

While we waited for the show to start, the house band were doing middle-of-the-road orchestrations of half a century's worth of pop tunes. You haven't lived until you've heard the same musicians play a bossa nova and a tribute to The Smashing Pumpkins. Various couples got on stage to dance to the mostly inoffensive rhythms, but I thought it would be rude to leave Abe by himself. I also wanted to be able to intervene should the cocktail waitress come back to take his order.

Abe, however, was watching the dancers with some interest. "On Brogard, you know, married couples don't think it appropriate to act like that in public."

"Really? Do you find it offensive?"

"To the contrary," he said to Larissa, "I find it rather refreshing."

"Would you like to dance?" Great. Now they were going to leave me here. Where did that cocktail waitress go? She could take my order.

"No, I don't think so," he said, just as the music stopped.

A much-too-cheery individual in a tuxedo took command of the now-empty stage to introduce the evening's entertainment. The big show was on Saturday night, but there was a singer and comedian in the nightclub every night. Today was Thursday. I hadn't heard of either of them. The singer was of the sort that, if she had been a supermarket product, she'd come in a plain box with the words "Musical Entertainment" stenciled on it. She had the sort of generic blandness that made me forget what song she was singing while she was singing it.

The comedian was even worse. No doubt attempting to amuse a mixed human/Brogardi audience was tough, especially since cultural exchanges had not yet begun and we had no real concept of the full range of Brogardi humor. Prematurely balding, and wearing a suit but no tie, he was carrying a cigar which already marked him as behind the fashion curve. He began with some jokes about the hotel, which were greeted with some laughs and wheezes, suggesting that our humor was more alike than one might have imagined.

"The emcee told me not to do any blue material, but I said, 'My best jokes are about the Brogardi.'" The drummer gave him a rim shot, while a frantic murmur could be heard in the audience. Had he given offense?

"What does 'blue material' mean? Was he going to wear jeans?" asked Abe, echoing in variation the question asked across the club. After several more minutes of this, I leaned over and asked Abe and Larissa if they wanted to leave.

A table to the side and away from the spotlight turned out to be just the right thing.

We had a pleasant enough week, with hearty meals, plenty of swimming and other activities, and Abe continuing to play "Stump the Bartender." After our first week, Larissa left to head back to L.A., but Abe and I continued to remain in hiding. One morning after an early breakfast, he went back to his room while I headed to the pool. I figured I had some time for the steam room and a quick swim before he was up and around again.

An hour or so later, I was climbing the stairs from the indoor pool to the main lobby, when I saw it mobbed. Ordinarily, I'd assume some star had arrived, but that was my Hollywood mindset.

"What's going on?" I asked the couple behind the jewelry counter tucked in a corner of the lobby.

"Big, big check in. Some sort of Earth/Brogard scientific conference."

I squeezed my way through the edge of the crowd and into the hallway leading to the Kennedy Wing. Bellhops were racing back and forth with carts, empty or full depending on their direction. The lobby would be impassable for some time to come.

When I got to the room, there was a note slipped under my door. "Jake—I'm at the nightclub. See you at lunch. —Abe." I had no idea why he'd be at the nightclub at 11 A.M., but this was exactly the sort of thing I was trying to avoid. My problem now was how to get to the nightclub on the other end of the hotel, when the lobby looked like the premiere in *Day of the Locusts*. As I left the room, I spotted one of the chambermaids. Since I'd have to tip her, too, I thought I should demand some extra service.

"Excuse me, is there a way to get to the nightclub without going through the lobby?" I knew I could go outside, but the front of the hotel was just going to be the automotive version of the lobby.

"Sure," she said with a smile, "You just go down that way." She pointed to where the Kennedy floor connected back to the main building.

"This way?"

"You go," she repeated, pointing.

I raced down the hallway, decorated more austerely than where we were, dodging the remains of room service trays and the occasional luggage-laden bellhop. At some point I'd have to go downstairs and face the lobby, but perhaps this would get me through the worst of it. I passed one staircase that led right to the center of the hotel—I could hear the roar of the check-in—but there was still plenty of hallway left, so I kept going. At the far end was a bend, and a few steps, and then another hallway, this one much brighter. At the end of this new hall was a door which opened onto a short flight of stairs. I was so disoriented now I didn't know where the hell I was. As I got my bearings, I was startled to see that I was a just a few yards from the nightclub. I was thoroughly confused. I suppose I should have been grateful that I hadn't run into a caretaker wielding an axe, like in some Stephen King novel.

The nightclub was dark, as one would expect in the morning, but the stage was all lit up. There were about a dozen somewhat elderly people— and Abe—getting a dance lesson.

"And one and two and cha-cha-cha, and three and four and cha-cha-cha."

Abe's partner was a woman on the sunny side of 70, clearly having the time of her life. Abe seemed to be concentrating on getting the steps right, but he had an expression that I knew meant he was having a good time.

"We're not taking reservations until 3 o'clock," said the woman at the *maître d*'s station.

"That's all right," I replied, "I'm just here to meet a friend."

Return from Witch Mountain

I slipped out of the nightclub before Abe spotted me.

He was acting responsibly. He was simply having a good time. I had to remind myself that everything was new to him. I suppose I'd be the same way on Brogard, getting all excited over something which Abe brushed off as no big deal. One day after breakfast I introduced Abe to one of my childhood vices: pinball. The kids were mostly playing the various video games, and we had one pinball machine to ourselves for most of the morning. Neither of us was very good, but we had a great time running through a couple of rolls of quarters.

We still had a few days to go when we got news that cut the trip short. It was late afternoon, and we were sitting at our usual places in the lobby bar. By now, a few regulars would stop by to see what Abe would order each day, getting the same for themselves. Business was so good that the bartender said Abe's drink was free if he had to look it up. They'd make it up in the dozen or so orders that came in after Abe got served.

"Jack and soda for the boring white guy and for my pal, Abe?"

Abe seeming to be awaiting the imaginary drum roll that was occurring in his head before he issued the day's challenge. Finally, he grimaced, which by now everyone knew was the Brogardi version of an Earth smile.

"I'd like a Widow's Kiss, please."

Behind us, a matronly woman leaned over and grabbed him around the neck. "Of course you would, *boychik*. Are we going to rumba, tonight?"

Abe looked up. "Hi, Millie. I'm saving the first one for you."

She squeezed his cheek. "You're such a cutie," she said, and then waved good-bye as she continued through the lobby.

I was beyond being surprised. "Abe, I don't know how you do it. It's a wonder that the owners haven't offered to make you Social Director."

Meanwhile, the bartender put down a drink that didn't look like anything I had ever seen before. "It's on the house, kid. I remembered the applejack, the chartreuse, and the bitters, but I forgot the Benedictine." He looked at me. "Damn, he's good."

"Widow's Kiss. That's with a 'W,'" I noted. "Does that mean we're nearing the end of the book?"

Abe wheezed and took a sip. "Not at all. What makes you think I'm doing this in alphabetical order?"

"I can dream, can't I?"

Abe was about to respond when we heard a voice calling him from the entrance to the retail arcade at the edge of the lobby. "Abi? Abi Gezunt? Is it really you?"

Abe looked up. Walking over to us, wearing a bathing suit and a T-shirt that read, "Brogardis Do It Interdimensionally," was a Brogardi of some years, if I was any judge of how they age. As he approached, Abe recognized him. "Behayma? What are you doing here?"

Abe and I stood up to greet Behayma, who reached out with both hands palms up. Abe greeted him in similar fashion, and then they both wheezed together. "Another Widow's Kiss," he said to the bartender, before turning back to Behayma, "You're going to love this."

"Who's your friend?" replied Behayma, looking at me with some suspicion.

"Oh, I'm terribly sorry. Behayma, this is Jake Berman. I have some business with him in California, and we came here for a break. Jake, this is Behayma Oyrech. He's my mother's brother. That would make him… what's the word?"

"Your uncle?"

"No… Yes, that's it. Uncle. Uncle Behayma." Abe said the word several more times, as if tasting it to see if he really liked it. "Behayma is my uncle," he said, finally.

Behayma pulled over a chair from one of the lobby tables so that he could sit between us. "So, Abi, what sort of business do you have in California?"

I answered. "He's advising us on Brogardi music. I understand he studied it at school."

Behayma looked at his nephew. "That Southern Continent stuff? You think they'll go for it on Earth? Personally," he confided to me, "I find it unbearable."

"But Behayma, you haven't told us what you're doing here. What brings you to Earth? And what news do you have from home?"

"I'm here to take some classes. There's a medical symposium here about adapting Brogardi medicine to the introduction of anesthesia. Abi, these last few seasons have been incredible. Do you know I can walk down the street now without having children run and hide, or their older brothers throw rocks at me?"

Abe answered my unasked question. "Behayma is a surgeon. Traditionally, it has not been a very honored position."

"You don't know the half of it," added Behayma. "Here on Earth, surgeons are considered great healers. On Brogard, children are frightened into obeying by being told that the surgeon will come to get them if they don't do as they're told."

"And have you seen my family?" Abe pressed.

"Everyone is doing just fine. I promised your mother I'd let you know how much she misses you if, by chance, I ran into you. And now here you are. I suppose you'll be having dinner with your father tomorrow night?"

"My father?" This last caught Abe and me by surprise. "I thought the Ambassador was back on Brogard on official business," I said.

"Yes, he certainly has been. After meeting with the leaders, he made his worldwide report to the people. I turned it off after a while." He looked at me. "No offense, Jake, but I'm not really interested in what he learned about your zinc mining operations."

"None taken, Behayma. To tell you the truth, I'm really not interested either."

"Another round, and this one's on me," announced Behayma to the bartender. "I insist."

Abe nodded, but I knew that the imminent arrival of his father meant that we would be leaving soon.

I slipped away while they were catching up on family business, and stopped by the reservation desk. Bonnie, the night manager, greeted me. "Hello, Mr. Berman. Did Abe get his free drink today?"

We had come here to be anonymous. Instead, Abe's presence was all anyone could talk about around the hotel. Maybe the arrival of the Ambassador was a blessing in disguise. It was time to go.

"He did it again," I answered. "I was wondering if you had the schedule for the Concord Spaceport. We wanted to check the arrival of a flight from Brogard tomorrow."

"Five P.M."

"I haven't told you which flight."

"Doesn't matter. There's only one a day. They say that when tourism and trade picks up, it'll be a regular Port Authority over there, but right now, there's the outgoing flight at 9 A.M. and the incoming one at 5 P.M."

"No exceptions?"

"There haven't been yet. Would you like me to call and confirm? What's the name of the person you're expecting?"

"Never mind," I said. "You've been most helpful. Can you arrange for our bill to be ready tomorrow morning? We'll be leaving after breakfast."

From my room, I made the arrangements for our transportation back to New York by car, and to L.A. by jet. Abe and I would fly separately, so as to avoid alerting anyone we might happen to run into who might recognize me and start putting two and two together. I also called our New York offices to have space available for me to handle the logistics for the premiere. As long as I was going to be in town for the day, I might as well accomplish something.

Before dinner, I filled in Abe about our change of plans. He seemed to be relieved. A public confrontation with his father was the last thing we wanted right now.

I gave Abe plenty of space after dinner that night. Behayma left for the Concord, where he was staying, to prepare for his medical symposium. And Abe said good-bye to each of the bartenders at the lobby bar and in the nightclub, thanking them for their hospitality.

I turned in early, but I understand there was a brief party after the late show, with just Abe and the bar staff. They raised a toast of a concoction made with Frangelico, a hazelnut-based liqueur, which had previously been called "Abbot's Delight." Henceforth, at the Raleigh, it would be "Abe's Delight."

We slipped out early the next morning. The plan was to drop me off in downtown Manhattan, and then get Abe and all the luggage checked through at the airport. This way, I could just hop a cab and head straight out without worrying about suitcases. At least we would be traveling in style. I had arranged for complete limo service, which meant that we had beverages and snacks on board, and that the driver was cut off by a soundproof partition from anything we had to say.

We had come too far now to blow it all with an overheard offhand remark. Drivers are notorious gossips, and many are tipsters for one newspaper columnist or another. It was exactly that attention to detail that had led Junior to hand me this assignment, and I intended to make sure his money was well spent.

It was about a two-hour trip into the city, and Abe spent the first half lost in silence. He seemed a little sad about having to go.

"Feeling blue?" I said, hoping the weak pun might get a reaction.

Abe waved me off, but then turned from the window, looking as if he wanted to say something, but didn't know quite how to begin. Finally he said, "Is that how Earth people typically have a vacation?"

What an odd question. "Well, there's no such thing as a 'typical' vacation. Some people prefer the mountains, some prefer the seashore. Some like lots of activity, some like sitting around doing nothing. It doesn't always involve as much drinking…"

"You seem to have a great deal of emphasis on fun and fantasy, instead of facing reality," he said.

"I'm not sure I know what you mean."

"Well, yesterday after lunch, I walked into the sundry shop and looked at the book rack. They had a sign noting the current best sellers. They were divided into two categories: fiction and non-fiction."

"So?"

"Well, why don't you call it 'fact' and 'non-fact' instead? The implication is that 'fiction' is the norm and reality is the exception to the rule."

"I hadn't really thought of it that way before…"

"And the dancing. There was no point to it. You just go in circles, doing different steps to different rhythms, but there isn't any purpose to it."

"I thought you enjoyed dancing. You certainly did enough of it."

In fact, Abe was dancing around the subject right now, but I figured I better let him get to what he had to say in his own good time. A good publicist has to know when to be the diplomat and when to play hardball. This was a time to step back. "Well, I did enjoy it… but my father would never have approved. He's very old-fashioned that way."

"Don't you have dancing on Brogard?"

He made a face. "It's what you would call folk dancing. Strictly for festivals and family occasions. And when it comes to boring music, I personally think we have it all over the Southern Continent. If you were to look up the word 'dull' in an English/Brogardi dictionary there would be a picture of Veyez Meer there."

"All right, I'll bite. Who is Veyez Meer?"

"Only the greatest composer the Western Continent ever produced. You actually have someone who sounds very much like him on Earth. I hear his music all the time."

"Really? Who is it?"

"I don't know what his name is, but he apparently does the music that they play on elevators."

This wasn't getting us anywhere. Abe was in a bad mood, and it wasn't because he was exposed to a lush arrangement of some ten-year-old heavy metal hit. "It's your father, isn't it?"

"What's my father?"

"The reason you're depressed. The reason you were so relieved when I told you we were leaving the hotel early. The reason, unless I miss my guess, that you came to Hollywood and Graham Studios in the first place. Tell me I'm wrong." There was a long silence, and I had the uncomfortable feeling that, perhaps, I had gone too far. Even the best of friends are supposed to know there are certain times to look the other way. "I'm sorry if I said something that's none of my business…"

"No, what you said was the truth, and that is what a friend is supposed to speak. You're right. Something has been bothering me."

I reached into the passenger fridge and pulled out a bottled water. I offered one to Abe, which he declined. He was ready to talk, and didn't want any distractions. "I'm here to help if I can, Abe, you know that."

"I don't know what sort of image you have of Brogard, but there are some events in our recent history that you should know. You're aware that it took a number of seasons after the initial receipt of your Earth signals to locate their source and decide how to respond?"

"Not really, but I assumed you guys didn't learn how to speak several Earth languages overnight."

"Well, your broadcasts couldn't have arrived at a more poignant time. We were in a global debate about our own culture, our mores, and our accepted ways of doing things. This was not a mere generational thing, like an Earth teenager defying his parents. This was a philosophic division that, if left unchecked, could have at the very least destroyed our world government. At worst, some people believed, we were on the road to war."

This was heavy stuff, and I had no idea what this had to do with Abe and his father, but I knew this style of storytelling. It was the way Larissa told me what happened in court that morning. Her anecdote would begin with the Code of Hammurabi and end, several millennia later, with some witticism she and her judge had exchanged. Abe would get to the point in good time. I just sipped my bottled water, and let him continue.

"The arrival of the Earth signals—especially as they increased over time, and we were able to figure out what they were, and examine them properly—were a revelation. We weren't alone in the universe. Our own differences seemed petty by comparison."

"I can certainly understand that," I said. "Your own arrival here had much the same effect on Earth."

"But our problems weren't resolved, they were simply put aside as we began the long, arduous tasks of learning your languages, perfecting the interdimensional drive, and trying to figure out if and how we should attempt to contact your world. Beneath the surface, the differences remained."

"It seems to have worked. Your father came here, Earth got over its initial shock, and now Brogardi can rumba with elderly widows at Catskills resorts."

"You're thinking like an Earthan, Jake. It's one of your most endearing traits."

"Thank you... I think."

"You Earthans tend to be result-oriented. If it works, then don't worry about it. We Brogardi are much more concerned about process, how we get there. The destination itself is relatively unimportant."

"Sounds like Buddhism."

"There are similarities, but the differences are significant. But let's not go too far afield here. Try to see it from our perspective for a moment. Suppose you were to see a Brogardi performance, what questions would you have?"

I gave it some thought. Since we hadn't yet begun any cultural exchanges, only those who had gone to Brogard had actually seen their entertainment. I assumed Junior or someone at the studio was studying the reports, or had even gone to Brogard, checking out what we might want to acquire for Earth distribution when the time came, but that wasn't my department. "I don't know, Abe, I suppose my first question would be how I would understand a foreign language."

"Okay, let's say I've taught you Brogardi, or we create a machine that translates the broadcast into English. Now what?"

"Let's see. I'm watching a Brogardi show. I can understand the language. What else do I need to know?"

"Exactly."

"Well, is it a series or a special broadcast? Are these continuing characters and, if so, how much of the past story do I need to know to understand what's going on? Is this a newscast or documentary, or is this the movie of the week?"

"Stop right there. That's the difference between Earth and Brogard in a single question."

I was confused. "Is it the movie of the week?"

"No, whether the story being told is true or not. It never occurred to us that you would be broadcasting lies about Earth…"

"Lies? It was *I Love Lucy*, not propaganda meant to mislead Brogardi."

"Of course, we understand that now. But we didn't really know that for sure until after we made contact. Our scientists and researchers had more information than they could sift through in a dozen lifetimes, and there was no way they could look at everything, or even select things in any meaningful order. It was all looked at randomly, and no one ever stopped to ask if the stories we were translating were accurate depictions of Earth history or not. There were serious debates as to whether all the conflicting stories could possibly be true. Your science fiction especially baffled us. If you had space flight, why hadn't you come to Brogard?"

"It must have come as quite a surprise to realize we weren't quite that advanced. But what does this have to do with your father?"

"While all of Brogard united on the Earth project, life went on. The debate over traditional ways versus trying new things continued, albeit on a lower scale. Those, like my father, who favored the traditional ways, argued with those, like myself, who wished to change and adapt to new times. Contact with Earth seemed to promise the opening of an entirely new era for us."

"And your father was sent as Ambassador…"

"Precisely. It was a compromise. By sending him, the transference of Earth ideas to Brogard was guaranteed to happen at a slow and measured pace. It's one of the reasons that the scientific and technology transfers occurred quickly, and there have been no exchanges of literature or music."

"We assumed you already had much of that stuff from the broadcasts…"

"Indeed, but that was really beside the point. It was the ideas that were expressed that my father's faction wanted to control."

There was something that didn't seem quite right here, like when you look in a mirror with a flaw and you can't figure out what's wrong. "All right, but if your father and his allies wanted to prevent Brogard from being infected with Earth ideas, why initiate contact in the first place? And why allow free travel afterward?"

"Contact was inevitable once we discovered you. And so was our traveling to you and allowing Earthans to come to Brogard. We are not a dictatorship where a leader tells us what we can or cannot do. Every individual is allowed to make their own search for truth. My guidebook says you have something like that here on Earth."

"We promise life, liberty, and the pursuit of happiness," I said. "If you want truth, you're on your own."

"Exactly. While my father doesn't want to encourage the wholesale exposure of Brogardi to Earthan ways, he recognizes that individuals may choose to come to Earth, or meet with Earthans on Brogard. It's the power of mass communication he fears, not the individual pursuit of truth."

"And it's your philosophical differences with your father that's the cause of the tension between you?"

Abe sat back in his seat. "I think I'd like that water now." I handed him a chilled bottle, which he opened and immediately drained. "It's a little more complicated than that, but that's certainly at the core of it."

I wanted to press Abe further, but the window separating us from the driver slid down. "Excuse me, Mr. Berman. We're at your Fifth Avenue destination."

Abe would make his 2:13 flight without any trouble, unless he started asking them why they couldn't leave at 2:12 or 2:14 and got airport security up in arms. Meanwhile, I headed upstairs to the offices of Woodrow "Woody" Jackson, senior vice president in charge of promotion and publicity for Surety Supermarket Supplies, the division of our parent corporation that had reserved Radio City Music Hall on our behalf. His secretary had me take a seat in his office, and said he'd be right back.

I glanced around the room, and took in the furnishings. They were a bit more conservative than mine, a bit richer looking, but more understated. It was the difference between being an executive in New York and being one in Hollywood. The people we dealt with were impressed by different things. On the walls were framed posters—seemingly originals—of concerts featuring Duke Ellington and Cab Calloway. Nice conversation pieces.

"Jake, it's good to finally meet you in person." I rose and turned, and greeted the six-foot-four executive whose office I was in.

"You must have been some basketball player," I said, shaking his hand.

"Indeed, 'some basketball player' is right. I was a total klutz. Two left feet, and I couldn't get the ball in the basket with a stepladder." He laughed to show he took no offense at what was clearly an assumption he had been fighting most of his life. I thanked him for his help, and then got down to business. I wanted him to bring me up to speed on the Radio City arrangements.

"It's like I told you on the phone, we got everything we asked for, except their union insists their own people must be employed."

"You told them we were trying to keep things under wraps?"

"They insist that their people can be trusted, and will not allow their replacement," said Jackson. "How serious a problem is that?"

"Very." It could blow the whole deal. We'd need most of the day to set up the theater and check the projection booth, and that would mean that any one of dozens of people could call the papers or TV stations with the "scoop." It also meant that the film would be run by a house projectionist for a theater that hardly ever showed movies any more. We simply could not allow that.

"I thought as much. That's why Colin Burns, the business agent for their union, is coming over in about twenty minutes. I told him I wasn't authorized to make any further concessions, and he'd have to speak directly to my boss."

"Boss?"

"I assumed you didn't want him to know you work for Graham."

"Woody, you did great."

"Does that mean you're going to let me in on your little secret?"

"Not a chance," I smiled. "But when I send you the block of tickets for your office, make sure you peel off enough for your wife and kids. This is going to be a night you won't want to miss."

Burns was about 30, showing up in the Surety conference room in a jacket, but no tie. It was the sign of labor: no matter how far removed they were from actual physical work, they still dressed as if they were ditch diggers and rail splitters. I was introduced as Woody's "boss," Mr. Berman, and Burns was all business, brushing aside offers of refreshment and of small talk.

"I'm here to listen, Mr. Berman, not to schmooze. You're trying to violate our collective bargaining agreement, and we will not allow that."

Woody started to speak, but I held up my hand. "Mr. Burns, speaking hypothetically, what would you do if I were to offer you, say, $200,000 to look the other way, so that we can run this event the way we want to."

Burns didn't even flinch. He looked me square in the eye and said, "I'd accept. Then I'd contact the NLRB and the FBI, and come back for the payoff wearing a wire."

Woody was shocked at this exchange, but kept quiet. Burns was waiting to see if I'd take him at face value, or look at this as hardball bargaining for a bigger bribe. I took his measure and made a decision.

"Colin—if I may?—I'm very happy you said that. You're an honest man, and you're looking out for the interest of your members."

"That's what I get paid to do—Jake." There was no hint of warmth there.

"Here's what I'm prepared to do: I will commit to paying your full shift of workers full pay, provided that they take the day off. I will also commit to our replacements being union members who will be paid the same amount, regardless of whether our agreement with them specifies less. I will further make the confidentiality agreement binding on both sides, so that no one else has to know that your workers were paid off for the day. In return, I ask for your cooperation and your silence."

"This must be some secret refrigerator you're demonstrating."

"I'm giving your workers everything they're entitled to, plus the day off. Do we have a deal?"

Burns hesitated just a bit. "And you're willing to put all this in writing?"

"We can have a binding contract ready by—" I looked toward Woody "—the close of business tomorrow." Woody nodded.

"I don't like this," he said. "It's an insult to our workers. Why aren't they good enough for a little trade show, when we handle everything from holiday spectaculars to international music awards to major concerts?"

"My reasons have to remain confidential at this time. Will two hours additional at time and a half apologize for the insult?"

Burns sat back in his chair. "I don't know what your game is, but like I said, I'm here to look out for my members' best interests. If I turned down an extra vacation day at full pay plus a bonus, they'd have my head."

"Then we have a deal?" I said, extending my hand.

"We have a deal," he said, grasping it.

"It's a pleasure dealing with an honest man, Colin," I replied, as Woody looked at the two of us and shook his head.

In terms of a typical movie budget, I'd just spent what amounted to an especially lavish premiere party. Considering our typical budgets, *The Brogardi* would be a little more expensive, but not by much. I couldn't help but think of poor Abe, though.

Those "net profits" he was entitled to were looking more distant than ever.

Invasion of the Body Snatchers

I was so jet-lagged when I got home that Larissa and the kids said hello, gave me hugs and kisses, and put me to bed. At some ungodly hour the next morning, I awoke and realized we were only a few weeks away from one of the biggest movie premieres of all time. David O. Selznick already had Atlanta on his side when he opened *Gone with the Wind* there. After all, he was bringing Clark Gable and Vivien Leigh along and adapting a best seller by a local author. We were going to New York and trying to create an event with no advance buildup except our "It's a secret" teaser campaign, which was old news by now.

It was only 6 A.M. when the guard waved me through the front gate. I figured I would have a few hours to go through the mail and memos that had piled up, as well as review what my staff had come up with for the campaign for *The Brogardi*. No matter how brilliant it was, I knew that there was nothing they had drafted that couldn't stand improving. After all, that's what I was getting paid for. I had stopped along the way to get a thermos of coffee and a bagel. No one would be in for quite some time, and I was willing to "rough it" in exchange for some quiet time.

"Good morning, Mr. Berman," chirped Betty, as I walked into my office.

I nearly dropped the thermos. "Aaaah! What are you doing here?!"

Betty didn't bat an eyelash. "Don't be silly, Mr. Berman. I work here."

I won't say that my heart stopped at the surprise of seeing her in the office, but I'll swear on a stack of *Variety*s that this new streak of gray in my hair arrived at precisely that moment. When I was able to breathe normally again, I looked at my watch. It was ten past six.

"Betty, you should be home in bed. You're not due in for another three hours."

"Abe stopped by yesterday when he got back on the lot. I was just getting ready to leave, when he popped in and said you were returning sooner than expected. I figured you'd want to get an early start. Was I mistaken?"

"No, Betty, you're right, as always."

She smiled with a little too much satisfaction for my taste, at least at this hour. "Now, I've sorted everything out. This pile is all the material on *The Brogardi* and the premiere, which I assume you'll want to get to first. This pile is mail and memoranda considered urgent. I put the trades and the less urgent material on the coffee table for you to look at later."

I looked at the stacks on the coffee table and shuddered, but it reminded me I had my thermos. "Let me just get some coffee…"

"Of course, Mr. Berman. I've just brewed a fresh pot of your favorite blend. Let me get you a cup. Will there be anything else?"

"You didn't make me a complete breakfast?" I asked, somewhat in a daze.

She smiled. "Of course not."

"Well, I…"

"I ordered out. It'll be here in about half an hour. I figured you'd want some time to go through some of the material before eating. Now, let me go get you your coffee."

"Betty, whatever we're paying you, it's not enough," I said, as she turned to head out to the reception area.

"Oh, it certainly is, Mr. Berman," she said.

Now I was really frightened. Who was this woman posing as my secretary?

The first thing to deal with was poster art. We needed at least three different designs up front, with more if—as we hoped—the picture had legs and settled into a long run. The first one was for one purpose: to decorate Radio City Music Hall on opening night. It had to be a poster that let people know what they were seeing without giving anything away. It was a glossy black sheet that simply said "Graham Studios presents *The Brogardi*" in bright, blue letters. It was actually a bit misleading, because there had been several documentaries about last summer's events that had been rushed into release, and such was their quality that most of the video copies sat unopened on shelves around the country. When nearly everyone had been recording the historic events, who needed someone else's version?

The next poster, to be unveiled the next day, was for the platformed opening, and would be used as a tease in theaters slated for the wider release. It was the same design, only now instead of the black background was a half-tone head and shoulders photo of Abe. He offered a three-quarters profile and a neutral expression. He looked powerful and mysterious, but intriguing rather than threatening. I okayed both.

The third one had to be a joke. It was a picture of Abe and Linda Reid superimposed on a shot of Earth from space. The copy across the top read, "Their love tore apart two worlds." Well, this poster certainly would. I X'ed it out and jotted in the margin, "Are you folks out of your minds? Class. Prestige. NOT sex."

The press kits and photos weren't a problem. The bio of Abe focused on his education on Brogard and mentioned that, yes, his father was indeed the Ambassador, and the rest of it was the usual boilerplate about what a wonderful production it was and how everyone admired Abe so much and how Caroline thought he'd be the first big Brogardi star in Hollywood.

I drafted a brief letter to the critics for Junior's signature, talking about how proud he was to continue his father's tradition of wholesome family entertainment, while being the first to welcome one of Brogard's favorite sons to Hollywood. It was unusual to have anything but the most impersonal cover letter in the kits, if even that, but then, this was an unusual film, and a note from Junior signaled that. Junior would add several paragraphs before approving it, which I would then take out, and this way we'd all be happy. So far the only hold-up was the video clips, because the film was still being edited and scored, but the people in charge said they'd be ready to ship by opening night. To be on the safe side, we'd have a stack of kits and video clips for the press who attended the premiere.

Betty popped in with breakfast—a western omelette, whole wheat toast, and half a melon—while I went through the "urgent" messages. I'd be on the phone most of the day dealing with this stuff, but *The Brogardi* had to come first.

"Betty, this is delicious. I'm not going to even ask how you knew this was my favorite. Please don't tell me. I'd prefer it to remain a mystery."

"If you say so, Mr. Berman."

"Next, it's only 7 now, but leave word with Sly's office to arrange for a meeting as soon as possible after he arrives."

For the next two hours I ate, drank, and dictated memos. I was nowhere near the piles littering the top of the coffee table, but I had managed to clear off most of my desk, so I was making progress of a sort. I was almost thinking of a nap when Junior's office called at 9:15. He had some time free if I could get right over. Great, he was raring to go, and I was already dead on my feet.

I hoped that Abe had gotten a good night's sleep.

Junior greeted me like a long-lost relative returned to the fold. I decided not to remind him that my nearly-two-week absence had been at his orders. Discretion is the better part of valor, and all that.

"Jake, my boy, I can see the vacation did you some good." He could? I felt like hell, and probably looked worse. Junior was of the old school. He believed that flattery would get him everywhere. "I've been here since 8:30, but I thought I'd give you some time to go through the pile on your desk before asking you over."

Really, Junior? I've been here since 6, and Betty parachuted in at midnight, after doing a black bag job for the CIA. No, Jake, this wasn't the time for sarcasm. Instead I was all business.

"I've reviewed the print materials, and I think we're in fairly good shape," I said. "One of the posters needs work, but that's for the general release, so we have time."

"Great. Now let's talk about the premiere."

Decisions, decisions. Did I tell him about my stint as a labor negotiator now, or should I wait until he had to pay the bill? I decided to wait. Let the premiere go off without a hitch, so I could use it as proof of the brilliance of my strategy. Right now, it would simply be an example of my profligacy. I was still waiting for him to challenge me on the Napoleon brandy.

"Radio City is all locked up, with our people entirely in charge top to bottom. We'll have a locked-door test screening that morning, to make sure the screen, projector, and sound system are all up to snuff. That gives us a whole afternoon for repairs and tweaking."

"Jake, you have been performing above and beyond expectations on this one. I've got another task for you, and I have every confidence you'll handle it with the same diligence you've shown everywhere else."

"Great," I said. Inwardly, I shuddered. At least I hoped it was inwardly. Fainting now would not be the best career move.

"I think we should invite Ambassador Gezunt to the premiere."

And in my spare time, why don't I invent a perpetual motion machine? "Sly, Abe and his father aren't on the best of terms…"

Junior was leaning against THE DESK. I was sitting on the couch along the wall, fighting the urge to put my head between my legs. "I know. That's the beauty of it," he said.

"I must still be jet-lagged. I'm having a little trouble following."

"We get the Ambassador there, but we don't tell him what for, and we don't tell Abe his father is in the house. Afterward, we have them reconcile on stage in front of the cheering audience. Can't you see the headlines? *Life Imitates Art; Ambassador Cheers Son's Movie Debut.*"

It would more likely be: *Gezunt Vows Revenge Against Graham, Berman; Promises to Devote Rest of Life to Destroying Them.* "I don't know if that's such a good idea, Sly…"

"It's great. It can't miss. I saw the rough assembly of part of the film two weeks ago. There won't be a dry eye in the house."

"Hold on a moment. How are you going to convince the Ambassador to attend a screening of a movie starring his son, when we can't tell him it's a movie starring his son?"

Sly smiled. "See? That's why I knew you were the right man for the job. That's what I want you to figure out."

I wasn't going to wait for Abe's father to kill him. I was going to handle the job myself right now. The only weapon I had on me was a roll of breath mints, but who said I wanted this to be quick and painless?

"Why don't you just put him on the payroll, Sly? Then you can just order him to attend."

"No, I don't think that would work. It's probably against the law," he said, seemingly impervious to sarcasm. "But perhaps we could bribe him by making a big charitable donation. Is there a Brogardi War Orphans Relief Fund?"

Where was he coming up with this stuff? "You want to make sure he attends? Set up a fund that will bring Brogardi surgeons to Earth to learn our medical techniques."

That got a response out of him. "Surgeons? What do I want to give money to doctors for? They can afford to pay their own way."

"No, actually, most surgeons on Brogard have very little prestige. They're analogous to our insurance salesmen or members of Congress. It's not exactly illegal, but you certainly wouldn't want your daughter to marry one."

"Really?" said Junior, intrigued. "How do you know so much about it?"

"Well, when you've immersed yourself in Brogardi culture as much as I have, you get to know these things." That, and bending the elbow with Abe's Uncle Behayma.

"And this is a big cause with the Ambassador?"

"If you ever had surgery without anesthesia, it would be a big cause with you, too."

"Great. I knew you'd do it. Now, how do we arrange for the Ambassador's security, without calling attention to the screening?"

"I'll tell them to make whatever arrangements they have to through Woody Johnson's office. He's been our beard on this from the beginning, and no one is going to look for a scoop about supermarket freezers."

"I don't have the vaguest idea what you're talking about, Jake, but keep up the good work."

While Junior turned to walk around to the other side of THE DESK, I beat a hasty retreat.

Junior's secretary told me I could probably find Abe over in the Foley suite, working on his footsteps. The notion of Abe walking in place in time to his recorded image was too funny to let pass. Besides, after four hours of adrenaline and caffeine, I needed a break.

It was a short walk over to the recording stage, where the Foley artists ran, walked, and otherwise moved over various surfaces, trying to match the sound to the picture. It was not the most fascinating work in the world, but it was necessary. I stepped into the production booth, and could hear a gentle skritch, skritch as I saw Abe walking on a small, carpeted platform on the sound stage. The Foley director saw me and nodded. Then he leaned into the microphone, "That was great, Abe. That's a take. We've got another two hours to go, but why not take five to stretch your legs?"

"Because they already reach the ground?" said Abe, his voice coming through the booth's speaker. There was stunned silence in the booth, shortly broken by Abe's distinctive wheeze.

"It was a joke, fellas," I announced.

"Oh. Very good, Abe. Very funny. You've got a visitor."

I went through the door to the sound stage, but the first person to greet me was not Abe.

"Daddy! I'm going to be in a movie!" Susan ran over to me and gave me a big hug. "Abe got me into the movie."

"Susie, what are you doing here? And what's this about you being in a movie?"

"Good morning, Jake. I see you got back okay." Abe came over and gave me a friendly pat on the back. "I tried calling you this morning, but Larissa told me you had left early. Since Susie had a vacation day today, I asked if it would be all right if she came over and kept me company."

"Well, that explains what she's doing here," I said, picking her up, "But what does she mean about being in the movie?"

"Daddy, listen. They needed a little girl to walk on the floor, and so they let me do it."

"I understand she'll be paid the day rate," added Abe. I looked at her. "You know nobody will be able to see you?"

She looked at me like I was hopelessly behind the times. "Abe said it will make me seem more mysterious."

I don't think she even understood what that meant, but she clearly liked the sound of it. It also meant she was now part of the big "secret project" her friend Abe had been working on all these months.

I put her down, and she ran over to a wooden platform and ran around on it. "Daddy, let me show you what I did."

We watched her run around for a minute, and then she came back. "That was very good, honey. I'm very proud of you, and I'm sure Mommy will be, too."

She took a moment to wallow in this praise, and then looked up at me. "Daddy? I don't think I have anything to wear to the premiere."

The Colossus of New York

It had been about six months since I first met Abe, and now, at last, we had come to the moment of truth. In just a few hours, *The Brogardi* would be unspooling before more than 5,000 invited guests. Word had inevitably leaked out that Graham's "secret" film was being unveiled that night, but it couldn't be helped. After all, if we were inviting the film press, they had to know what they were going to be seeing, and if it was worth their time and effort.

Once the invitations were out, it was public knowledge. Besides the critics, there were also the major theater owners, film bookers, and various business associates who had to be included. I sent a hundred tickets to Woody Jackson with a big thank you. Another hundred were sent to Colin Burns "with the compliments of Graham Studios." With the veil of secrecy being lifted ever so slightly, I thought they were entitled to see why Radio City Music Hall was being four-walled, as if it was a small-town movie house rented out by a traveling revival meeting.

At the last minute, Junior had the brainstorm of inviting the President of the United States, but I explained to him that if we invited her, we'd have to invite the heads of state of all the other members of the UN, reminding him of the marathon "welcoming speeches from hell" session that the Ambassador had been put through last summer. We settled for the Mayor, the Governor, and a truckload of Senators and Congressmen. There was one son of a bitch from South Carolina who had called for new Congressional loyalty hearings against the movie industry a while back, and I thought it was only fair to return the favor. I personally mailed his invitation out the day of the premiere. I expected it would arrive some time next week. I felt it was the least I could do.

The film was finally locked down about ten days before the opening. There was a private screening held for Junior, Caroline, Abe, and myself. Everyone else would have to wait for the premiere. My job, ostensibly, was to select the scenes we would put on the clip reel for the TV reviews. Even the trailers were going to be different from the usual "scenes from the movie" ads that we usually did. After the premiere, we'd run some silent footage while quoting the most laudatory reviews from the most prominent critics. There'd be no "rent-a-blurb" ads from those so-called quote whores, who say whatever you want just to see their names in print. There was one guy who was so pathetic that we called him whenever we wanted a "This is the movie of the year!" quote to promote one of our turkeys. At last count, he had named close to twenty films "the movie of the year," and we hadn't even hit the summer yet. We weren't even bothering to invite him to the New York screening.

The only thing that remained an unknown was the film itself. Except for Abe, even the principal cast would have to wait for the premiere, and the crew would get separate invitations to the L.A. opening. As a courtesy, the director of photography was invited to the New York screening, but declined because he was in the middle of some historical epic in the Pacific Northwest. He promised to make it down for the L.A. show.

So now the four of us sat in the dark, waiting for the film to begin. The Graham moose bellowed, and then the stark credits ran against the backdrop of space. The only credits that would appear at the start of the film were these: "Graham Studios presents A Sylvester Graham, Jr. Production of a Caroline Sosniak Film" and "*The Brogardi*." Everything else would appear at the end. This kept the mystery going a little while longer.

The opening consisted of brief clips of the landing in the Catskills, and the cheering of the Ambassador's speech at the United Nations. The screen faded to black, and then the superimposed title "One Year Later."

Until this moment, there was no way to tell where this movie was going. Now it began to unfold. What we saw was a small stage that, we were informed, was in Rochester, New York. Abe gave me a nudge.

"I hope Larissa's father won't mind," he said.

Onscreen, we had moved into a small theater, which was holding tryouts for a regional production of *A Midsummer Night's Dream*. In the audience, the director and a few others were reviewing their choices, when an aide came over and whispered in his ear, "We've got one more."

"Show him in," muttered the bored director, clearly going through the motions. Cut to the bare stage, where Abe was about to audition for a part.

The director sits up and takes notice. "He's a Brogardi. What the hell am I going to do with him?"

This led to the tryout scene that I had seen shot the day of the wrap party, and we were off to the races. To my amazement, the movie turned out to be good, surprisingly good. Abe was able to project his essential decency and goodness, making us really want his character to succeed. When his screen father rejected him, it was heartbreaking, and when they were reconciled at the end, I really did want to cheer. When the lights came, up I looked down at my notepad: it was empty. I had gotten so caught up in the melodrama that I had forgotten to jot down the scenes I wanted to excerpt. That wasn't a problem. I could do it from memory. The point was that if this movie affected me, a jaded industry veteran, what was this going to do to Mr. and Mrs. Moviegoer?

Junior had been right after all. We had all become part of something that was very, very special.

"Abe, you may have come out here as a Brogardi," I said, "but you're going back a star."

Whoever said that getting there is half the fun never traveled with the Berman family. Even Elizabeth was coming on this trip. Let's see: we were flying out today and would have a quiet family dinner in our hotel room tonight. Tomorrow, I'd spend all day at the theater, overseeing the preparations, while Larissa took Susan and the baby to one of the museums. Later, we'd hire a baby sitter for Elizabeth, while Larissa and Susan would join me at the theater for the premiere. Afterward, we'd be having a very small dinner party, since the big premiere bash would be held in conjunction with the L.A. opening. The idea was that we wanted to focus attention on Abe and the film, not on the glitterati at some New York soiree.

I had packed a suit, a couple of shirts and ties, the usual socks, under-wear, pajamas, toiletries, and a guidebook called *Welcome to Brogard* that I had finally asked Betty to get for me last week. Better late than never. This came to one suitcase. As we gathered in the hall to make our exits, I noticed that next to my lone suitcase were ten pieces of luggage.

"Dear? Why do you need ten pieces of luggage for a two-night stay?" I thought this a perfectly rational and reasonable question.

"Because we need everything, and I've already compacted it as much as I can," Larissa replied.

I found this hard to believe. "I find that hard to believe," I told her. I picked up one bag. "What's in here that's so important?"

"That happens to be Susan's clothes."

It was bigger than my bag, but a child needs some extra clothes in case she drips ice cream on herself, or falls down and rips something, or any one of dozens of unforeseen possibilities.

"And Mr. Bunny," Susan piped up.

"Of course." I put that bag aside with mine. That left nine.

"Now, what's in here that's so important that we can't be without for two days?" I hefted the bag. I assumed it contained a complete workshop of tools, including an anvil.

"Elizabeth's formula."

My temples started to throb. "Let me get this straight. We're carrying a bag full of baby formula to the other side of the country? New York's in a different time zone, not the Third World. Why don't you just take enough through tomorrow morning, and buy what you need in New York?"

She looked at me as if I had just gotten off the boat. "Now where am I supposed to get baby formula in New York?"

"I don't know. Where do you get baby formula here?"

She ignored my question and fired back with another of her own. "And what if they don't have her brand?"

"She's ten months old. She can't even read. She doesn't have brand loyalty. Give her something else. She'll never know the difference."

"I don't have time for this," Larissa answered. "We're taking the formula."

The next three bags were also Elizabeth's. They contained diapers—another commodity that was apparently scarce in New York, toys, and clothes. The clothes bag was nearly as big as Susan's, and she wasn't even going to the premiere. That meant that the remaining five suitcases were all Larissa's.

I knew she could justify every single thing she had packed—in her own mind, at least—and it was pointless trying to dissuade her. Once, an hour before a dinner where I was a featured speaker, I tore a seam in my suit pants. Larissa smiled very sweetly, and reminded me that I had told her that she didn't need everything she had packed. Her sewing kit was in the bag we left behind. I had to tip the concierge $50 to get the pants fixed in time. Since then, I only make symbolic attempts at getting our accumulated luggage down to some reasonable weight.

After an uneventful flight, we arrived in Manhattan and checked into our hotel a couple of blocks from the theater. We were all there except for Abe, who was in a smaller, more elegant establishment several minutes away. Junior had told him to start getting used to star treatment, but it was really one last effort to misdirect the media. By now, it was public knowledge that we would be opening our film the next night, and Junior was known by enough people to make him a target for the cameras. With Abe in relative seclusion, no one was likely to connect him to us.

As chief publicity honcho, I was under special pressure to feed the press which was starving for information and, after months of secrecy, was getting downright surly. A few days before, *The Ducklings' Brogardi Adventure* hoax had apparently been laid to rest when one of the cast members was hospitalized for gall bladder surgery. A family friend told a reporter from one of the tabloid shows that the actor hadn't worked in months, but had been looking forward to the next Ducklings film, set to begin production in the fall. Junior was fit to be tied, but cooler heads prevailed, and a fruit basket was sent to the hospital with a note wishing him a speedy recovery and hoping that he'd be working with us again real soon.

I'd gotten both Abe and Junior tickets to Broadway shows that night, more out of self-defense than out of some need to keep them amused. I wanted a night off before what was likely to be the most hectic twenty-four hours of my life. With both of them separately entertained, I could enjoy a quiet evening with my family. As it turned out, it was one of the few things I did right.

The calls started at seven the next morning, with everyone looking for the exclusive as to what the "secret" film was about and who was in it. I instructed the hotel to forward all calls to the theater, which would at least protect Larissa from having to deal with the ravenous hordes. When I arrived there at eight, they had just completed installing the new movie screen, which we had arranged in partial payment of what we owed for the use of the theater. It gave us something to exploit, and anyone who called was faxed a florid three-page press release extolling the virtues of the state-of-the-art screen in SuperGigantoMax that represented a commitment of Graham Studios to the finest in motion picture presentation.

There wasn't a word in there about *The Brogardi* or Abe or even the fact that we were staging a premiere that evening, but it was something, and it gave the various entertainment reporters who needed to file by noontime something to write. We even provided a twenty-minute window for camera crews to come in and film the gigantic screen. Reduced to a TV picture, it wouldn't seem like much, but with the hungry maw of the media demanding to be fed, it was a morsel.

By eleven, it was time to test the system. Several technicians scattered around the orchestra level while I took a perch in the first mezzanine. The houselights dimmed, the curtains opened, the Graham moose came and went, and the titles appeared on screen: "Graham Studios Presents *The Ducklings' Brogardi Adventure.*"

I sat up in disbelief. What followed was a mix of news footage and outtakes from previous Ducklings movies, including a scene that made it look like the Duckling family was asking the questions at a press conference held by Ambassador Gezunt.

"Pretty funny, huh?"

I turned around and saw Caroline in the row behind me with a big smile on her face. "What is this?" I asked.

"It's our test reel. I worked with a couple of editors to throw this together after the *E.T.* story broke. We never got to use it, so I brought it along to test the projector and sound, rather than risk the real film." She looked around the cavernous theater. "It's a big place. No telling who's around."

"All right," came a shout from the floor, "It's a go." A few muffled voices reacted to the shout, and then the film stopped and the lights came up. We stood up, and could see our chief engineer on the floor. He gave us a big thumbs up.

Behind us, a door slammed open, and Diane ran in. "Jake, there's been a leak." It was Diane who had saved us in the *E.T.* fiasco, so I was instantly alert. I attempted to shake off Caroline, but she made it clear she wasn't going anywhere. Well, she'd know soon enough anyway.

I told Diane to calm down. We both took a deep breath. Then I asked, "What happened?"

"Right after the projector test, I spotted somebody at the back of the theater. When I went over to see who it was, he jumped up and ran out. I found this." She handed me a little black plastic box. It was a video cassette box, and inside was a sticker labeling it the property of one of the syndicated tabloid shows. I handed it to Caroline.

"I am so sorry," Diane was continuing, "I should have run faster and tried to tackle him…"

Caroline put a sympathetic arm around her shoulder. "Dear, it's only a movie," she said, then turned and walked away.

She left it to me to put poor Diane out of her misery. I told her what we had just seen, and to make sure that the show's rivals were invited over for an exclusive interview with Junior this evening, right after the film began.

I do love my job.

At three P.M., we began setting up for the buffet in the lobby. The lobby of Radio City Music Hall is one of the seven wonders of the entertainment world (how Rob Schneider keeps getting work is another), and we would be running a major league cocktail party there from five until seven. The movie was set to roll at eight, and most of the invitations suggested people arrive at 7:30, but the film press and selected guests were invited to enjoy the special courtesy of the open bar and what were amusingly called "heavy hors d'oeuvres." As far as some of these people were concerned, this was dinner.

At 4:30, we sealed the building. No one was leaving now until after the show, and no one was getting in without our permission. I gave Diane the go-ahead, and the stark opening night posters began appearing on easels around the lobby and on the landings of the grand staircase. Since the cost actually shrunk per unit once the presses were rolling, I had ordered several thousand posters, even though we only needed about a hundred at most. At the end of the evening, we would give each attendee a poster as a souvenir of this historic event. Ordinarily, we would do a specially bound program, but that would give the whole show away before the movie even started. We gave posters away at sneak previews all the time, but I suspected these would become treasured heirlooms. I pulled a dozen for myself and put them aside. You never know when you might need to bribe someone.

A few minutes later, Larissa arrived with Susan. Susan had been told that she was not to mention Abe's name at all tonight, because that's what their secret was all about. After again extracting a promise that she could bring him in for show and tell, she said she'd be good. However, she said, we'd have to keep an eye out for Mr. Bunny, a notorious chatterbox. But when she got her first look at the ornate lobby, even Mr. Bunny was speechless.

Junior arrived a few minutes later with his wife, Sylvie, in tow. Larissa knew her obligation was to be the dutiful wife tonight, but she knew she'd get even at the national court reporters convention in Chicago in August. She and Sylvie helped themselves to some champagne from a passing waiter, and then took Susie over to the concession stand for a lemonade.

"Caroline told me about the spy this afternoon," was Junior's greeting, once we were alone. "That was a close one."

I told him my idea for revenge by speaking to their rivals, and he heartily approved. I knew that Junior could never bear to look at any of his studio's films more than once, and sometimes not even that much. No doubt he'd be pacing the back of the theater most of the evening, gauging the audience reaction, but having seen it, he had no problem with taking calls, doing interviews, or heading to the bathroom to throw up, depending on how the screening was going.

Caroline and her husband also arrived. He was an anthropology professor, of all things, and found his wife's milieu fertile ground for his study of primitive tribes, or so he told us. Half the time, I couldn't understand what the hell he was talking about, and the other half he looked like I was speaking in some tongue unknown to him, so we tended to smile on those occasions when we were required to be together, all the while looking for an escape route.

As the clock brushed past five, one set of doors was opened, and those with the appropriate gold-trimmed invitations were admitted. It was about five hundred people, or around ten percent of our expected movie attendance, and each of the Graham people had those key guests they had to meet, greet, and coddle. My job was the national press, who knew they were seeing a movie called *The Brogardi*, and what the intended release dates were, and nothing more.

Across the room, I spotted one of the TV duo who had wheedled their way into our critics comedy several months ago. He was loading up a plate with crudités, and I avoided making the obvious pun. After all, I wanted to keep these guys happy.

"So, is it true it's really my movie you're showing tonight, and all this *Brogardi* stuff is more of the same gag you've been running for weeks?"

His movie. If it was a hit, he was going to be demanding gross points. "What are you talking about? We're holding your film back for the fall festival season. We're going to be showing it in Toronto and Boston, unless we get invited to be the opening night film in New York."

He suddenly looked pale. "I thought it was just a goofy comedy."

"Well, there've been some changes since you and your partner filmed your scene." I let him sweat a moment. "C'mon, I'm just pulling your leg. It opens on two thousand screens on Fourth of July weekend. It's going to be the comedy laugh riot of the summer, and everyone's going to be raving about what a good sport you are."

He was still giving me the fish eye. "Good sport?"

"Well that, and how film criticism's gain is the movie industry's loss."

I patted him on the back and sauntered off. I figured it would be quite some time before he deconstructed that sentence and figured out just what I had said.

His partner was standing before one of the easels, examining the poster. Since it revealed nothing more than he already knew, he seemed to be giving it much more attention than it deserved. Perhaps he was hoping it would be one of those "magic eye" things with a hidden 3-D image suddenly revealed.

I sidled up to him. "I think the kids will like it."

He looked at me in horror. I had uttered the code phrase indicating that the movie was a bomb. No publicist could bad mouth their own studio's product but, on the other hand, we wouldn't last long if we shamelessly flacked each release as if it was the greatest story ever told. After all, in a week or so the movie would be gone, but our relationship with the press would continue. Thus, the promise that kids would enjoy a film was a way of signaling what was really going on without saying anything that could get the publicist in trouble if it were ever repeated.

"You rented Radio City Music Hall for a…" He looked at me closely. "Very funny, Jake. You almost had me there for a minute."

We exchanged a few pleasantries about how, of the hundred or so movies already released this year, there was nothing worth seeing, and then—spotting his partner across the room—he headed in the opposite direction. I turned and found myself facing Larissa, who was holding a glass.

"Drink me," she said. "You're wired. And when you're wired, you get giddy and do silly things. You're the only one I know who sobers up the more he drinks."

At 6:30, the coffee and dessert trays were brought out, and by seven, the food service—except for the concession stands—was closed, right on schedule. Now the doors were opened, and the floodgates released. Our premiere audience began to arrive in earnest.

I spotted a few Brogardi in the crowd, but not many. Except for the Ambassador and his entourage, we had stuck with friends and business associates, and they were all from planet Earth. However, we had put no restrictions on guests, especially to those whom we had given blocks of tickets, so it wasn't surprising either. We had arranged with the Brogardi Embassy to allow them to enter shortly before showtime through a service entrance. Pleased by the generosity of Graham's scholarship fund, the Ambassador had agreed to attend, but only on the condition that he not be set up to seem to be endorsing the film.

Our other Brogardi was Abe himself. He had been slipped in quietly during the cocktail party, and was relaxing in a dressing room behind the stage. Given that the area often has to house the Rockettes and several other groups of performers, there was no lack of space. Larissa, Susan, and I slipped away to see Abe, who would be escorted to a seat in the theater just as the film began.

"So, Abe, ready for the big night?"

"Daddy! Shh! You're not supposed to say his name," shouted Susan.

"It's all right, dear," said Larissa, "We're in private now."

Abe picked up Susan and gave her a big hug. "I'm so glad you were able to come," he said. "I made your Daddy promise he'd bring you to the opening." Abe offered her his "happy" grimace, which even she was able to recognize by now.

"Elizabeth is here, too, but she had to stay at the hotel because she's only a baby," she informed him, with due seriousness. "I'm allowed to stay up late because I'm a big girl."

"You certainly are," he said, putting her back on the ground with a grunt. I wondered if he had been getting his massages.

I gave him his instructions for the evening. "We have a seat on the aisle for you, about ten rows back. Right after the houselights come down, Diane will bring you to your seat. After the film, she'll escort you to the stage."

"We've been over this already. Relax, Jake, you're more nervous than I am," said Abe. He pulled a bottle of champagne from an ice bucket set up in the corner, and poured out enough for the three of us. "Sorry, Susan, this is grown-up stuff."

"I know," she pouted, occupying herself showing Mr. Bunny the dressing table.

"Good luck," said Larissa, clinking glasses.

"It's beyond luck now," I said, after taking a sip. "Now it's up to that special something that turns just another studio production into movie magic."

"As one of your Earthan philosophers said, 'There's no business like show business.'" Larissa and I both looked at him. "I got the quote right, didn't I?"

There's something special about a premiere. There's an air of expectation. Only a handful people know what they're about to see in its finished form, and the audience wants it to succeed. All except the most jaded movie critics hope each time that this one will be special, and join the pantheon of great films that live on in our collective subconscious. Even people who've never seen *The Jazz Singer* know Jolson's line "You ain't heard nothin' yet," and Claude Rains' protestations in *Casablanca* that he is "shocked, shocked" about the gambling at Rick's Café Américain has become the definition of hypocritical cynicism. Would *The Brogardi* turn out to be another great one, or merely one of the hundreds of films that are made and forgotten each year, doomed to collect dust on store shelves until sold at bargain rates to make way for the newer failures? To be at the premiere means to be able to say forevermore that you were there at the beginning. Now it was time to find out: the beginning of what?

Larissa and Susan took their seats, and I joined Junior at the back of the orchestra level. As the house lights dimmed and the curtains parted, I saw a door on the side open, and Abe being ushered to his seat. If anyone wondered why this Brogardi had arrived late, they quickly forgot as the movie got underway.

Somewhere upstairs, Ambassador Zetz Gezunt was being escorted to his private box. He had asked to be allowed to arrive without fanfare, and we made sure that he and his party could get to their seats without attracting attention or running into Abe, who was similarly avoiding the crowds.

Junior and I had plenty to do during the screening, but there was one moment that we wouldn't have missed for the world: that moment when the audience realized that the star of *The Brogardi* was a Brogardi. There were a few gasps, and I thought I heard a nervous giggle, but it was impossible to tell where in the huge theater it might have originated. As Abe began his audition, ten thousand eyes focused in on him. Everyone was trying to decide whether they could accept a Brogardi as a movie star. When he finished his speech and left the stage, it was clear that we had won the battle, if not the war. They were going to give him a chance.

I grabbed Junior and shook his hand. Then I hustled him out to the lobby for quick five-minute interviews with the networks, three cable services, and the syndicated tabloid show that hadn't tried to sneak into the theater this afternoon.

It was showtime.

Not of This Earth

Nearly two hours later, Junior and I were backstage, watching the credits roll by on the screen in reverse. Out front was a tremendous roar of approval. We had a hit. When Abe's name came up in the cast listing, the ovation doubled. The waves of sound were the sweetest noise I had ever heard in my life.

I peeked through the curtains. No one was running out. The invitations had said there would be a live presentation following the feature, but the credits would crawl by for a minute or two, allowing people to sneak out. Instead, they continued cheering.

At last it was over. The screen was raised up, and a spotlight was turned on. Junior walked out into the pool of light, where a microphone was already in place. From somewhere in the theater, an announcer introduced Junior to the audience.

"Ladies and gentleman, the producer of *The Brogardi* and the president of Graham Studios, Mr. Sylvester Graham, Jr."

More applause. Some cheers. You'd have thought this was the State of the Union address, with the politicians carrying on for several minutes before the speech could finally begin. This was no show for the cameras, however.

This was for real. Whatever the results from the critics and, ultimately, the box office, this audience tonight had been touched.

While Junior talked, two things needed to happen. Diane was stationed down front and off to the side, ready to escort Abe to the stage at the appropriate moment. Meanwhile, I was heading to an elevator that would take me up to the first mezzanine level, where I could fetch the Ambassador and let him know that his son was ready to meet him onstage.

I had already checked out the route in the afternoon, so I knew precisely where I was going. This place was such a maze that I could get lost and never find my way out. I was sorry that I didn't have a bag of bread crumbs so I could leave a trail in order to find my way back.

When I got to the door to the Ambassador's box, I could hear a new round of applause. Abe had just been introduced, and the audience was going wild. I opened the door, prepared to show my pass to any Brogardi security that might be stationed there, but I was able to walk right in. I was able to walk right in and take any seat I wanted, because the whole damn box was empty.

What the hell was going on here? Was I in the wrong box? Had they all felt the call of nature at once? Was this some kind of once-a-decade Brogardi mating ritual? No, none of my experiences with Abe had led me to believe there was anything unusual that would have led to a mass exodus. I must be in the wrong box. I turned around and raced into the hall, looking for someone who could tell me where they were.

I spotted an usher at the end of the corridor. It made more sense to speak to her than to start barging into every box and asking, "Yoo-hoo. Mr. Ambassador? Anyone home?"

"Where are they?" I shouted instead, frightening the poor woman out of her wits.

"Where are who?"

"Ambassador Gezunt and his party. It was about half a dozen Brogardi dignitaries. They're all blue. You couldn't have missed them."

"You mean in the first box?"

I'm about to have a heart attack and this woman is questioning seating arrangements. "I don't care where they were sitting. Where are they?"

"Oh, they left," she said, looking around to make sure she wasn't cornered.

"They left? What do you mean they left? The movie just ended."

She suddenly saw what the problem was. "They didn't stay for the movie. They left about five minutes after it started."

"They left?" I realized I was bordering on the incoherent. "How could they have left? Which way did they go?"

She pointed to the staircase behind her. I raced down the stairs, and found myself in the middle of the lobby. My staff was setting up tables to distribute the souvenir posters, as well as a table with press kits and video clips for the critics. They saw me coming down, and assumed I was here to check up on them.

"Where are they?" I screamed.

"Where are who?" answered the twenty-something stacking the press kits.

"The Ambassador and his party. Ambassador Gezunt. They left their box and came down this way."

"I've been here for forty minutes, Mr. Berman. No one's come down this way since I've been here."

I looked at the others. They were all nodding in agreement. I ran behind the concession stand and picked up the house phone. I called our operations office.

"Lyman," came the matter-of-fact voice.

"Dick, thank heavens. It's Jake. I went to get the Ambassador, and his box was empty. They tell me he left, but nobody saw him leave the building."

"Hold on, Jake." I heard him talking, and some static. "Jake, I've just radioed the garage. They say he left two hours ago, just after the movie began."

"Shit. Gotta go." I dropped the phone and went racing into the theater. I had to let Junior know what happened. We could worry about why the Ambassador had flown the coop later. I just didn't want to have the evening spoiled by Junior inviting him to the stage and being greeted with stone cold silence.

Abe was doing his first draft of his Academy Award speech, thanking everyone who had anything to do with the making of the film. No one seemed to mind. It was such an honest bubbling of enthusiasm that it came across as endearing. A star is born.

"...most of all, I want to thank Jake Berman, the senior vice president for publicity, who has become a very dear friend, along with his wife Larissa and his daughters Susan and Elizabeth."

Somewhere in the audience there was a shriek. "He said my name."

"It's okay, Susan," wheezed Abe from the stage. "It's not a secret anymore."

This got a big laugh, and I took advantage of the opportunity to race onstage and get to Junior's side. "Ladies and gentlemen, Jake Berman."

Huh? There was a loud round of applause, not like the kind that Abe had been receiving, but if you've never stood on the stage of Radio City Music Hall and had an entire theater full of people clapping at the sound of your name, you have no idea of what it was like. Me? I was frozen in place. I'm a behind-the-scenes guy, not the one in the spotlight. I didn't know what to do. All I could see were these bright lights and a vast sea of darkness. Up front, I was able to pick out faces, but I wasn't really able to focus. I waved at the darkness, and then turned to Junior. Ever the showman, he bailed me out, putting his arm around me and pulling me aside, smiling all the time.

As we slipped out of the spotlight, Abe began to wind up his thank yous and his expression of gratitude to the audience. Meanwhile, without losing his smile, Junior was giving me the third degree.

"Where's the Ambassador?" he whispered, just loud enough for me to hear.

"He wasn't there," I said, the panic rising again.

"Keep smiling, Jake. We're on stage, and there are 5,000 people watching us."

I smiled. I looked at Junior. He smiled. Then he grabbed me and pulled me off into the wings.

"What do you mean he wasn't there?"

"He left. Right after the movie began, Gezunt and his entourage made for the exit. Dick said they went straight to the garage and shot out of here like a bat out of hell."

"Why?"

"I have no idea. Maybe he thought he just had to make a perfunctory appearance. In any case, there won't be any onstage reunion with Dad tonight."

We both looked out at Abe, now bowing and waving as yet another ovation rocked the house. Somehow, I didn't think he would mind.

Dinner was a small but boisterous affair, in a private room of a restaurant near the theater. The glass doors were all curtained so that we had a vague sense of the restaurant, but were pretty much left in our own world. The party was primarily for Graham people and whatever family they had brought along, which meant several spouses and Susan. Except for Junior and I, no one else knew the details about the debacle with the Ambassador, so everyone else there was in a festive mood. Larissa could tell there was something forced to my hilarity, but wisely didn't press it. There'd be plenty of time to give me the third degree later.

As a joke, I'd had a dummy menu printed up in which every dish was broccoli. It was even funnier when Caroline's husband attempted to order from it, pronouncing the selections "refreshing." As I said, he was from a different world, one far more different than the ones Abe and I hailed from.

Junior was in no mood to speak, but I got him to propose a toast to Abe, and then announce that all the speeches that needed to be made that night had already been delivered from the stage. This meant we could relax, and Junior wouldn't have to pretend he wasn't concerned about something. He might be a brilliant producer, but he was a lousy actor.

At one point, Dick Lyman took me aside to ask what the story was, but all I could tell him was that we had invited the Ambassador to see the film, and were surprised that he had left early. It was really all I knew, but I didn't feel like going over the failed attempt to get him on stage with Abe.

At midnight, I was burnt out and ready to head back to the hotel. I'd been running on fumes for several hours now, having overseen the whole production since early that morning. Diane came over with a stack of the early editions of the New York papers. There wouldn't be reviews as such until the film began its regular run, but there were several news and feature stories about Abe's triumph on the silver screen. We even made the front page of the *New York Times*, albeit below the fold. No one had picked up on the Ambassador's presence or hasty exit, which was the best news I had had since discovering that he had left. Tomorrow, we'd all head back to L.A. to prepare for the West Coast premiere, and the major festivities there. This is where anybody who was anybody in the business would want to be, especially now that word would be out that we had the event movie of the year. Everyone would want to be among the first to see it, and maybe get a chance to sign up Abe for their next project. A nice dividend was that a lot of people would now want to bring their next projects to Graham, since we were suddenly the ones with the juice.

Abe came over and took the seat next to me, while Larissa was getting Susan ready to head out. He placed a hand on my shoulder.

"How are you doing, friend?"

"I'm exhausted. But the question is how you're doing. You may not realize it yet, but your life has been irrevocably changed. Starting tomorrow, you're no longer Abi Gezunt, itinerant Brogardi musicologist. You're Abe Gezunt, movie star. You'll be on the cover of *People* and

Rolling Stone, and everyone will want to know everything about you: why you don't like chicken, what you were like as a boy, who you're sleeping with…"

Abe turned away, and I could have sworn he looked guilty. "You haven't been seeing Linda again, have you?"

"I gave you my word, Jake. No one would see my blue skin next to hers except on screen."

"All right, then. When we get back, my suggestion to you is that you get an agent and your own publicist. You might hire a lawyer as well. You're going to need a platoon of gatekeepers if you're going to protect your privacy and control people's access to you."

"Why would I want to do that?"

I was very tired, and more than feeling the effects of alcohol, but I felt this was important. "Say you want to go with Susie to visit her class."

"I plan to. A promise is a promise."

"Okay, but why are you really going? What's in it for you?"

His eyes went wide. "Jake, I'm surprised. I told Susan I'd go with her months ago, as soon as the film was done and the secrecy was over. I'm actually looking forward to it."

"Abe, I believe you. I've come to know you, and I know that you would never lie to me. But all those people out there, they don't know you." I waved my arms vaguely, gesturing at the rest of the planet. "And when they see you do this, they're going to see a publicity stunt. Some will even accuse you of using an innocent Earth child just to promote your movie."

"But why will anybody see me? I'm just going to go visit Susan's class, not hold a press conference."

"That's why you need gatekeepers: so that the press is fed enough information so that they won't feel the need to invade your private time. You can't do it yourself, and if you tried, they'd eat you alive."

Larissa came over with a very sleepy Susan. I stood up and turned to Abe. "Have I ever steered you wrong, Abe? I don't know how they treat movie stars on Brogard, but here on Earth, you're going to need all the help you can get."

Abe stood and gave me a hug. Before he let me go, he whispered in my ear, "We'll talk tomorrow."

We said our goodbyes, and left the restaurant. All I wanted now was to get back to my hotel room and crawl into bed until it was time to leave. The sooner I had my back to New York, the better.

At five A.M., we were awoken by a pounding at the door. Our flight wasn't until noon. Who the hell could this be?

I opened the door to see a several uniformed soldiers. In front was their spokesman, whose nameplate identified him as "Col. Hashimoto."

"Mr. Jake Berman? Please come with us," he said, in a voice that made it clear that this was an order, not a request.

I wasn't even fully awake yet. "Excuse me? Are you sure you have the right room?"

"You're Jake Berman of Graham Studios?"

"Yes."

Hashimoto signaled to his men, who brushed me aside as they came into the suite. "We'll wait while you wash up and get dressed. You have five minutes."

"Now hold on just a second there," I said, grabbing his arm as he, too, strode into the room. He took my arm and quickly and firmly removed it. "Mr. Berman, you're in a lot of trouble. The President of the United States does not like to be kept waiting. I suggest you move it. You now have four minutes."

He hadn't hurt me, but the force with which he removed my hand made it clear that he could have—and would if he had to. I went into the bedroom and quickly dressed. I brushed my teeth, but didn't even bother shaving. If they're going to wake me up in the middle of the night, then let them worry about good grooming.

"What is it, dear?" Larissa was barely awake herself.

"I don't have time to explain. See if you can find Gretchen O'Hearn, and tell her that I've been summoned by the President."

"What does Junior want with you at this hour?"

"Not Junior. The President of the United States. And if they're coming for me, I suspect Junior already knows."

We marched down the corridor single file. First one of the armed soldiers, then Hashimoto, then me, then the other soldier. If this was a movie, I probably would have pulled off a daring escape, incapacitating all three of them at once. Since this was real life, as opposed to reel life, I marched right into the service elevator.

"Would you mind telling me what this is about?" I asked. Hashimoto had pressed the button for the garage, bypassing the lobby.

"The President wants to see you. That's all I know."

"Just me?"

"I wasn't given the list, just my instructions about apprehending you."

The list? Had that redneck from North Carolina gotten his late invitation and decided to stage a coup? Hashimoto refused to provide any more information, and I accepted the fact that he probably didn't have any more to offer.

I was led to a car, and got in the rear after one of the soldiers. Hashimoto took the passenger seat in front of me. "Don't think of trying to jump out at a red light. You won't get very far."

I didn't get what he meant, until we pulled out into the early morning light. Several jeeps were rolling along in front of and behind us. The only way I'd be getting out of here was if I could fly, and they probably had helicopters and even spaceships up there, for all I knew.

The cars sped east, racing through red lights which were purely advisory at this hour anyway. We were far away from any of the areas of the city I was familiar with, until I saw the site that was famous the world over, even if you're never been to New York.

We were going to the United Nations.

Earth vs. the Flying Saucers

I had been left sitting in some conference room for about twenty minutes, when Col. Hashimoto returned with two new guys in suits.

"Please sit down, Mr. Berman. You're in a lot of trouble," said the older of the two, evidently the boss. By this time, I had been building up a head of steam, and a let it out at once.

"No, whoever you are, *you're* in a lot of trouble. I'm an American citizen and a civilian and I have rights. I don't say another word until I get a chance to talk to my lawyer and somebody tells me what the hell is going on here."

The younger of the two men whispered something to Hashimoto, who nodded and left the room.

"No one's told you why you're here?" asked the older man, who had taken a seat at the head of the table and pulled a legal pad out of his briefcase. He adjusted it so that it was exactly perpendicular with the edge of the table, and then reached into his jacket pocket for a pen.

"Other than getting the bum's rush from your storm troopers, no one's told me a thing." There was nothing like righteous indignation to make one brave—and foolish. If I had thought about it, I would have realized I had no cards to play.

"Now, now, Colonel Hashimoto was just doing his job. Did he hurt you? Were you injured in any way?" He was solicitous to the point of being grandfatherly. Meanwhile, his partner had pulled out a tape recorder, and was performing the same geometric maneuverings his partner had with the pad.

"Don't good cop/bad cop me. I want some answers."

"As do we, Mr. Berman. Your rights—if they are at issue—may well be suspended in wartime."

"Wartime! Are we at war? With who?"

"That's what we're going to find out. I want you to tell me all about your relationship with Ambassador Gezunt and his family," he said calmly, nodding to his assistant. The younger man hit a button on the tape recorder and adjusted the microphone so it was exactly between them, facing me. "Start at the beginning."

Two hours later, I was telling the story for the fifth time. After my initial bravado, I realized that I did, indeed, have one card to play: spin control. I could tell from their questions that my interrogators didn't know a thing about the movie business, and I told them what happened in a way that put Graham Studios, and me, in the best possible light. After all, we hadn't done anything wrong, and there was no reason for me to feel guilty.

As I became more cooperative, I was able to get some information out of them, too. Junior, Caroline, and Dick had also been picked up this morning. Gretchen O'Hearn, the studio's general counsel and the person who might have been most useful to me if Larissa had been able to reach her, was the one who got away. Rather than stay for the dinner and the overnight in New York, she had left right after the premiere. Apparently, half the FBI was blanketing Southern California looking for her, but she had thus far eluded their net. Either that, or she had snuck away for a couple of days off, not realizing she was the subject of a nationwide manhunt.

When they started asking me to tell the story for the sixth time, I lost my cool again. "I have nothing further to say. I have told you everything you wanted to know *several* times, and now I want a shower and breakfast. After that you can execute me as an intergalactic spy or release me, but you're not getting anything else out of me."

My two interrogators—who had yet to tell me who they were or who, precisely, they represented—exchanged glances. Then the younger one began packing up the tape recorder, while the older one flipped back the pages of his now-filled legal pad. He then returned his pen to his breast pocket, and placed the pad back in his briefcase.

"Thank you for your cooperation, Mr. Berman. We'll be in touch." With that, they left the room.

I was alone again, and still hadn't even been offered a danish and a cup of coffee. I went to the door to see if it was locked, but instead it swung open again, and there was Colonel Hashimoto, who now had four guards with him.

"Come with me, Mr. Berman."

"Where are we going?"

"You'll find out soon enough." And that was the last I got out of him.

I lost track of the elevators and corridors we went through, but since it was only 7:30 in the morning, I wasn't surprised that the offices we passed were all dark and empty. At last, we came to a huge room with a big circular table in the center surrounded by rows of chairs. It was some sort of amphitheater, with this big table being the focus of attention. There was a group of chairs set near the front portion of the table, and I was led to one, while Hashimoto and his men moved off to the side. Shortly, I was joined by Junior, Caroline, and Dick, who each arrived separately with their own military entourages.

"Is everyone all right? Did they tell you what was going on?" asked Junior.

Dick, the ex-Marine, had clearly been most at ease with the situation, speaking the same language as the people who were escorting him, if not necessarily his interrogators. "Ambassador Gezunt called the Secretary-General around 3 A.M. in a rage. He's threatening to break off diplomatic relations with Earth, and possibly worse. When they asked him what the problem was, he told them it was our movie."

"What? How could he threaten to go to war over a movie?" asked Caroline.

"Especially when he didn't even see it, or his son," I chimed in.

"So that's what that was all about last night," said Dick, suddenly putting the pieces together. I quickly filled in Caroline about what had been planned with Abe's father, and what had actually happened.

"I guess this means Abe's publicity tour of Brogard is off," said Junior.

Before I could smack him on the side of the head and point out that if we went to war over this movie *nobody* was going to see it, the doors at the front of the room opened. In strode the President of the United States. As the other delegations came in, I spotted the Russian President and the British Prime Minister, and I assumed that the other nations had sent their head honchos as well. I wouldn't have recognized the Governor-General of the Solomon Islands if I had tripped over him in the street, so I couldn't have sworn that he was there.

There had been some major callings on the carpet in the course of human history, but this one was apparently going to top them all.

Colonel Hashimoto ordered us all to be seated as the various delegations took their places around the table. There were a group of empty seats at one end of the circle, to our immediate right. When everyone was in place, the Secretary-General gave a nod, and the doors to the rear of the chamber opened. In walked a dozen Brogardi, headed up by Ambassador Gezunt. At the back of the group, to our amazement, was Abe. He gave us a little wave and shrug of the shoulders, but there was no telling what that meant. I waved back, just to be on the safe side. The Brogardi group took their seats, and then the Secretary-General rapped his gavel.

"This special meeting of the United Nations Security Council is called to order. Due to the extraordinary nature of this meeting, I will be presiding." He looked around the room to see if anyone had any objections. No one did.

"We are here to try to avert a crisis and to fix responsibility for this matter," he continued, glaring at our group, which pointedly did not have a place at the table. "Ambassador Gezunt, you have the floor."

Gezunt rose, decked out in full, formal Brogardi drag. He turned and looked at us, before facing forward and addressing his remarks to the other delegates. He had a big, toothy smile on his face.

"This shouldn't be so bad," said Junior, who was suddenly acting relieved. "He looks like he's in a pretty good mood."

"It's worse," I hissed back. "The only time the Brogardi show their teeth like that is when they're really, really angry."

"We're in deep shit," muttered Dick to no one in particular.

"We are an honest people," said Gezunt to the delegates, "who seek the truth in all that we do. We have come to you honestly and openly, in friendship. And this is how you repay us. You heap insult upon insult, disgracing my family and then, and *then* have the audacity to invite me to wallow in the filth with you. Never in the entire history of my world has such an outrageous and grievous assault on our sensibilities ever been recorded. We have been in conference all night, and it appears we have no choice but to immediately abrogate all treaties with Earth, and to declare your planet irredeemably hostile to Brogard."

The chamber was in uproar. Some of the delegates were waiting for the simultaneous translation to end, so they could figure out what he was going on about, and even then, most of them appeared confused.

Obviously, something horrible had been done to besmirch the honor of Brogard, but Gezunt had failed to specify what, exactly, it was.

Gezunt now turned to Abe, who was seated behind him. "Abi, my son, how could you disgrace your mother and I this way? I could not believe my eyes when I saw your 'movie' last night." You could actually hear the quotes around the word movie.

"Mr. Ambassador," interrupted Junior, "My name is Sylvester Graham. I don't want to mix into any personal business, but I run a quality operation. My movies are fine family entertainment…"

"On your world, perhaps," replied Gezunt, with a withering glance.

Junior didn't give an inch. "You only saw a few minutes of it. How would you even know what was in it? In fact, it's being hailed this morning as a tribute to your people and your friendship with Earth. I'm sure it will be just as warmly received on Brogard."

"No!" shouted the Ambassador, slamming his hand down on the table. "This abomination will never be allowed to appear on Brogard, as I'm sure Abi could have told you."

We all turned to Abe. "I'm sorry, Sly. If you had asked me in the first place, I would have warned you not to invite my father."

"But what's wrong with being an actor," asked Graham. "It may not be as important as being an Interstellar Ambassador, but it's certainly no great crime."

"It is on Brogard," replied Abe, in a voice so low we could barely hear him.

"Mr. Ambassador," said the American President, with some trace of exasperation, "What seems to be the problem? After all, it is only a movie."

"It is a work of fiction!" shouted Gezunt, to the shocked silence of his party. The rest of the room was similarly stunned. A couple of the delegates were tapping at their earpieces as if they were afraid they were getting a defective translation.

With every eye in the chamber now upon him, he continued. "I apologize for my choice of words, but they apparently cannot be avoided here. The tellings of such false tales is expressly prohibited among those who have any claim to be part of civilized society on Brogard. Only the worst sorts of degenerates pay any attention to them or," he added, glancing at Abe, "appear in them."

Abe rose to his feet. "I'm sorry you feel that way, father," he said, apparently discovering a sudden reserve of strength, "because that is not the Earthan way. I like what I'm doing, and I'm going to continue."

"Then I have no son," said the Ambassador with finality. He then did something I had heard figuratively, but had never seen literally: he physically turned his back on his prodigal offspring.

"Now hold on there just a moment, Mr. Ambassador. I've never seen someone acting like such a big horse's ass in my life!" Everyone looked around the room to see who would have the audacity to address the Ambassador in such terms, knowing the result could mean interplanetary war, or worse. To my shock and amazement, it was me.

"Mr. Berman, that will be enough. Take your seat at once," shouted the President of the United States, having grabbed the gavel away from the Secretary-General.

"No, Madame President. I will not take my seat. I've had it up to here with being a pawn in the political maneuverings of two worlds. We make movies. Last time I looked, that wasn't against the law anywhere on Earth," I said, spinning on Gezunt, "which is where, Mr. Ambassador, you happen to be right now."

"A temporary mistake."

"No, Mr. Ambassador, the only mistake you've made is turning your back on your son."

"That is none of your affair."

"When I was woken out of a sound sleep and dragged here in the early hours of the morning, away from my family, it became my affair. You think your son did something wrong? You know nothing about him. Abe is the finest person I have ever had the privilege to meet. Do you know that he saved my daughter's life? Do you know that there is an entire hotel full of people in the Catskills who absolutely adore him? Do you realize that this movie"—I spat the word out at him—"is going to do more to help Earth/Brogard relations than any of your pompous pronouncements?"

"How dare you?!"

"No, how dare *you*. You're ready to go to war because your son has adopted Earthan ways? Do you think you're the first father who's ever objected to a son wanting a career as an actor?"

"My son has disgraced Brogard with his appearance in this movie. On Brogard, the only use for fiction is as a solitary sex aid. It is a profession for degenerates and perverts."

Holy cow. I suddenly saw Abe's video collection in a whole new light. No wonder he didn't want to see them in a screening room. He must have had a difficult enough time getting through the show last night. I quickly put that thought out of my head.

"Fine. So we won't be opening on Brogard any time soon. But let me tell you something, Mr. Ambassador. I know something of your ways, too. And if you attack my friend Abe—someone who I trust with my family and with my very being—then you're attacking me. And if you attack me, I will devote the rest of my life to making sure everyone on Earth and on Brogard knows that the reason this great friendship between our two worlds was strangled in its crib was because a pig-headed old fool didn't understand what a wise Brogardi once told me."

"What's that?" the Ambassador asked, barely holding his rage in check.

"When on Earth, do like the Earthans."

"Colonel Hashimoto," shouted the President, "Get these people out of here at once."

"Nice going, Jake," said Dick, as we were hustled out of the chamber. "You've probably just gotten us all shot."

Independence Day

We had been separated again, and locked in separate rooms. So far, no one had even offered me a glass of water.

"What now, more questioning?" I demanded of Hashimoto.

"Don't you think you've already said more than enough, Mr. Berman?" With that, he closed the door and locked it.

By noontime, I was ready to make a break for it. I was starving, and madder than hell. I started pounding on the door. Let them shoot me, but first they were going to have to feed me.

The door opened, and I began demanding something to eat. Hashimoto cut me off with a wave of his hand. "Mr. Berman, if you will come with me, please."

Now we were getting somewhere. Once again, Hashimoto and his troops ushered me down the hall to the elevators, but this time we were taking a simple route. We got to the lobby, and they escorted me right to the street, where a couple of jeeps had taken over a bus stop.

"I'm not going anywhere until I'm fed. And I demand my right to an attorney."

The soldiers got into the jeeps, except for Hashimoto. He turned to me. "Mr. Berman, you are free to go." He boarded the jeep and signaled the driver to take off. As the engine turned over Hashimoto said, "Good day to you, sir."

And they drove off. I was standing on the street by myself, watching the traffic go by. People were on their lunch hours, doing errands, oblivious to the fact that I had been—until just a few moments ago—a prisoner of the United Nations. Short of the loons who are still ranting about fluoridation being a Communist plot, I couldn't imagine a soul who would believe me.

Fortunately, I had my wallet with me, so I could afford lunch and a cab, in that order. It occurred to me to call Larissa to let her know I was all right, but for all I knew, she and the girls had taken the noon flight out of here as scheduled. There was certainly no reason to believe she had remained at the hotel. Unfortunately, my cell phone had remained there, plugged into the charger.

I needed a pay phone, a twentieth century artifact that had not yet entirely vanished. I slipped into the first coffee shop I saw. Fortunately, Manhattan has one on every other street corner. I found a pay phone in the back, and started punching in the three dozen or so numbers that were required for me to call my office and charge my studio account for it. It only took me four tries, a new personal best. I was hoping that, if anyone would know what was going on at this point, it would be Betty.

"Publicity and promotion, Mr. Berman's office."

"Betty, it's Jake."

"Oh, Mr. Berman. Thank goodness. The phone has been ringing off the hook all morning."

"I'll tell you about it after. I wanted to find out—"

"Oh, I already know, Mr. Berman. It's been all over the news. Ambassador Gezunt has formally withdrawn any protest or complaint against our film, and all of you were released. The President said Graham Studios may have averted the first interstellar war."

My head was spinning. Not two hours ago we were being accused of *starting* the first space war. There would be time to sort this out after.

"Betty, have you heard from Larissa?"

"Oh, yes. She's waiting for you at the hotel with Susan and Elizabeth. And I've rescheduled you for a flight later this afternoon. I hope that's all right."

"Betty, someday you'll have to tell me how you do it. It's more than all right. I'll check in later."

"But Mr. Berman—"

I hung up, and ordered a sandwich to go. I'd eat in the cab. I may have been in a hurry to see Larissa, but if everything was really all right, they could wait a couple of minutes longer, while they put together my hot tongue on rye.

"It's Daddy!"

Susan's shriek could probably be heard in all corners of the massive lobby, but I didn't care. I was ready to howl a bit myself. I ran through the lobby unshaven, without a tie, and with a mustard stain on my jacket from when the cab hit a pothole on the trip uptown. I literally jumped over a coffee table making the last few yards to my wife and daughters. I lifted

Susan up as the three of us embraced. It was exactly like one of those corny scenes in the movies where the refugees or the survivors of some disaster discover the others just before the credits roll. Well, they say every cliché has a grain of truth in it somewhere. Elizabeth waved her teething toy at me from her stroller. I gave her a big kiss on the top of her head.

"I was so worried, Jake," said Larissa. "They wouldn't tell us anything. And then when the news broke and they said you'd be all right—"

"What news?"

"About the funeral. Don't you know?"

"I've spent the last few hours being shuttled from pillar to post. Start at the beginning. Pretend I don't know anything."

"Well, I assume you know Abe's father was very angry about the movie."

"Yes, I was there for that. I also arranged for a blood feud between the two of us."

"What?"

"I'll explain later. The last I heard, the Brogardi were canceling all treaties and leaving Earth, since our warm, fuzzy film is apparently the Brogardi equivalent of *Behind the Green Door*."

"What's behind the green door, Daddy?"

"Never mind, Susan."

"We have green doors in the cafeteria at school," she continued, eager to be part of the conversation. I grabbed Mr. Bunny by the throat and held him to my ear.

"What's that, Mr. Bunny? You can't understand what Mommy's saying if Susan keeps interrupting?" I returned the doll to her. "We don't want to make Mr. Bunny confused, do we?"

"No," she said, a bit sulkily.

"Good. Because Daddy's already confused enough," I said, returning my attention to Larissa. "Dear, please continue. The Brogardi were about to declare war."

"Well, that's when the story broke about the funeral."

"Whose funeral?"

"Some French scientist. He was on Brogard, studying applications of their dimensional drive, when he keeled over and died. It was a heart attack."

I was getting more bewildered by the moment. "And we're blaming Brogard?"

"No, it was natural causes. It's what the Brogardi did afterward. The French delegation wanted to bring the body back to Earth for burial, but the Brogardi scientists wanted to show how bad they felt, so they insisted on preparing his body for transport."

"And that's why we're upset?"

"It's not what they did, it's how they did it. When the casket was examined before being loaded on the ship, they discovered that his remains had been…"

"Yes?"

Susan's desire to be part of the conversation could no longer be restrained. "They cooked him, Daddy."

"They what?!"

Larissa provided the details. "On Brogard, burial or cremation are considered wasteful. The way one honors the dead is by consuming their mortal remains. The Brogardi couldn't understand what the fuss was all about. According to their beliefs, their death rites are extremely spiritual."

I was straining to understand the full ramifications of this, when something clicked. "And I'll bet they say it tastes like chicken."

"Why, yes. How did you—" Larissa cut herself off in mid-question. "Of course. It's why Abe would never touch it. It reminded him too much of somebody dying."

"Mommy, I'm hungry, and so is Mr. Bunny."

Hungry? I was hoping I wasn't going to lose my lunch right there in the lobby.

"In a few minutes, dear. Let me finish telling Daddy what happened." This story couldn't possibly get any stranger. "The scientists got back yesterday, and waited until they returned to France to make the announcement. The story broke late this morning. The Brogardi were stunned by the reaction."

"No doubt. And no doubt the reaction on Earth wasn't one of praise for Brogardi thoughtfulness, either."

"In France, they were ready to declare war on Brogard. Fortunately, the UN Security Council was already in session, and Ambassador Gezunt was already there."

"And suddenly the shoe was on the other foot."

"Mr. Bunny isn't wearing any shoes, and he's getting very hungry."

I couldn't bear to hear very much more about food at the moment. "Dear, why don't you take the girls to lunch? Betty said our airline tickets have been changed to a late afternoon flight, so we have some time. I ought to find out what happened to Junior and Abe and the rest."

After another big embrace and lots of kisses, they took off for lunch, and I looked for a phone. Crossing the lobby, I passed a newsstand, where I saw the *New York Daily News*, which had put out an extra with the headline: "WAR AVERTED." Gezunt had made a brief statement around the time of my release, saying that it was important that our two planets respect our differences, no matter how shocking they might be by the others' standards. The story quoted Gezunt as saying that his advice to Brogardi shocked by Earth ways could be mirrored by the Earthans who disapproved of Brogardi practices. Said Gezunt, "When on Earth, do as the Earthans do. When on Brogard, do as the Brogardis do."

It sounded awfully familiar.

A few phones calls confirmed that everyone had been released. Junior was already on a flight home, while Caroline and her husband were heading to New England for a well-deserved vacation. Dick would be on the same flight as us back to L.A. Which left only Abe. The news accounts pointed out that Abe's appearing in our movie had become a *cause célèbre* on Brogard, but no one seemed to know where he was. On a hunch, I called Betty.

"It's Jake again. I've hooked up with Larissa, and we'll be leaving for the airport soon. What I wanted to know is if you've heard from Abe."

"Well of course, Mr. Berman, that's what I was trying to tell you when you hung up on me." She sounded almost hurt.

I quickly and humbly apologized. After all I had been through, I couldn't afford to have Betty angry with me. At this point, I couldn't rule out that it was within her powers to have me deported to Brogard.

Her feathers unruffled, she found his message in the apparently growing pile on her desk. I was not looking forward to returning to the office. With any luck, most of the messages would have been mooted by the news.

"He's checked into your hotel. He's planning on spending a few days in New York before he's due back here for the Los Angeles premiere. He's in room 1505."

My next call was to my favorite florist in L.A., where I had a large but understated bouquet delivered to my office.

I had the message read "Betty—I don't know how you do it!" I was going to leave it unsigned, but then I realized that she might think it was from Tom Jones, and that wouldn't do at all.

"Sign it 'Mr. Berman.' And add a P.S. 'You win.'"

I got off the elevator on the fifteenth floor, and tried to figure out which direction room 1505 would be, which was not as easy as it sounded. There were several banks of elevators serving the hotel, and the one that I had used dropped me off at the far side of the hotel, at the other end of the corridor. Through a few twists and turns, I finally located Abe's room, and knocked on the door. We would clearly have a lot to talk about, and it probably wouldn't hurt to find out if we had a budding film star, or a newly chastised Brogardi who would never appear before the cameras again.

When the door opened, I got the shock of my life. Standing there before me was the last man I expected to see: Sidney Nathan, my father-in-law.

Teenagers from Outer Space

"Sid? What the hell are you doing here?"

He gave me the oddest look, and then he did something I had never heard him do before. He doubled over and started wheezing.

"Abe, honey, who is it?" called a familiar female voice from within the suite.

"Abe?" I looked again. Peel off the grey hair and the California tan make up, and there was something awfully familiar about that face. I stepped forward, reaching for his collar. Pulling it back, I saw the telltale gills.

"Jake! Don't hurt him."

I had no intention of hurting him, but I looked up to see who was telling me not to do so. Standing behind Abe, looking rather appealing wearing a plush terry bathrobe emblazoned with the hotel's crest, was Linda Reid. She had been absent from both the premiere and the United Nations round up, but had now suddenly reappeared.

I didn't think there was anything coincidental about it, but I was having trouble thinking straight. At that precise moment, the lack of sleep, lack of proper nutrition, and lack of preparation for the series of shocks that had pummeled me one after the other since last night finally took their toll. I did the only thing a reasonably normal man could do under the circumstances: I crumpled like a cheap suit.

When I opened my eyes, I was lying on a couch, with a cold washcloth draped across my forehead. Abe was seated in a dining nook, which had been set up with an electric makeup mirror and various tubes and jars. He was busy wiping the gook off of his face. Linda was nowhere to be seen.

"I'm so sorry, Abe, I can't understand it. That's never happened to me before. It must be the jet lag or something…"

"Are you all right, Jake? I was starting to get concerned." He put down the washcloth, and came over to the couch.

"How long was I out?"

"Out? You were here the entire time."

"No, I mean how long was I unconscious?"

"Only a few minutes."

I sat up, and started to get my bearings. When Abe offered me a club soda out of the room's courtesy bar, I suddenly remembered why I had passed out. "What the hell were you doing, dressed up as my father-in-law? And where did Linda go? Did she leave, or is she already in the bathtub, getting your water the right temperature?"

Abe remained unflappable. "A promise is a promise, Jake."

"Yeah, it certainly is. What happened to that promise? You weren't supposed to be seeing Linda anymore."

"No, actually, if you'll recall, what I said was that I wouldn't let anyone see my blue skin next to hers, except on screen. Until you arrived here, no one has."

That took a moment to sink in. "You mean you've continued to see her?"

"Of course I have, Jake. We're in love."

"But you promised me. And this whole to-do with your father was because your people don't lie. What do you call this?"

"A partial truth?"

"What?!"

"It's just like you told me. Tell the truth, but leave out the part that the other person doesn't need to know." He had me there. It was exactly what I told him.

"All right," I confessed. "You got me. Besides, after the last twenty-four hours, I doubt if you and Linda doing a spread in *Penthouse* would raise an eyebrow."

"Whose penthouse?"

"It's a skin magazine. Never mind. But what's with dressing up like my father-in-law?"

Abe starting wheezing. "Well, remember at the wrap party, when I said you sounded like my father?"

"Barely." Having recently gotten into a shouting match with the Ambassador, it was a comparison I didn't relish making, nor one I found particularly apt.

"Well, when I began trying out different makeups, to see if I could pass as an Earthan, I noticed that with a little help, I had an uncanny resemblance to Larissa's father. I usually added something, so that people who knew him wouldn't make the mistake, but I figured I was in New York City, and he wouldn't be caught anywhere within a thousand miles…"

"So you just gave me one of the biggest shocks of my life, that's all."

Abe came over and sat next to me. "I'm sorry about that, but I was trying to do what you asked. And after my father nearly started a war…"

"Yeah, what the hell was that all about? Why didn't you tell me?"

"Why didn't you tell me that you were going to invite him to the premiere? How do you think I felt when I found him sitting in the lobby of my hotel when I got back from dinner?"

"Really? He was waiting for you? How did he know you were there?"

"Well, I could hardly come to New York, knowing I was going to be on the front page of every newspaper the next day, without at least letting my father know I was here. I hadn't even spoken to him. I simply left a message at the embassy that I was in town for a few days, and where I would be staying. We weren't close but we were still family—at least until last night."

Suddenly, I realized what all this had cost Abe. I had been so focused on the movie and the premiere that I had never stopped to think what it meant to him. He might never be able to go home again. If being with Linda offered him some solace, I sure as hell wouldn't complain any more. "I'm sorry, Abe. I had no idea…"

"I know that. It's like I've told you: our differences are much more interesting than our similarities. I don't think you'll have to worry about my father any more. He's almost certain to be replaced as ambassador."

"But what about you?"

"Me? Alone? Friendless? A pariah on two worlds?" He doubled over and covered his face with his hands.

"Abe, I feel so awful." I tried to think of how I could possibly console him, when I heard that telltale wheezing. He leapt up and waved his arms in glee.

"I don't! I'm a star!" He danced around the room, reminding me, of all things, of Susan after she had gotten a compliment. "Don't worry about me. I'm doing fine. And there are many Brogardi who feel exactly as I do, even if my father doesn't know it. Even if my mother chooses not to tell him."

"Your mother?" I didn't know if I wanted to hear this. Abe lowered his voice, more out of habit than anything else. "Who do you think gave me my first novel?"

A few minutes later, a fully clothed Linda Reid came out and, under Abe's watchful eyes, we kissed and made up.

"I think both of us were a little too quick to judge the other," she said. "I realize that you really did have Abe's best interests at heart."

"No, it doesn't matter anymore," I said. "You two are actors. As long as nobody gets hurt, the rules don't apply to you." I tried not to sound jealous, which I was, and failed.

"Well, I'd like to think I have higher standards than that," she huffed, but that was more reflex than anger. Smiling, she took my hand, "Oh Jake, anyone who cares for Abe as much as you do is obviously going to be a friend of mine. Since he got back, he couldn't stop talking about your confrontation with his father at the UN."

"You mean when I blew my stack and acted like a total idiot?"

"No, no, Jake," said Abe, "When you stood up, defenseless, against those in authority, and shouted out the truth without any fear of the consequences. Speaking truth to power is the most honorable act known to any Brogardi. Our greatest heroes in history have been those who said what they knew to be true, regardless of whether they would be punished or destroyed. What I saw you do this morning was, quite possibly, the bravest thing I've ever seen anyone ever do. And when I think you were speaking in my defense, saying what I wanted to say—"

"But you did speak up," I objected.

"Barely. I held back much of what was in my heart, because I was afraid of how he would react, not only against me, but against both our worlds. But you—you had no fear at all."

"He means I had no sense at all," I said to Linda. "Heroism comes from not thinking about what you're risking until after the fact," she said.

"Jake, I don't know how I can ever repay your act of honesty and friendship."

"Friends don't need bookkeepers, Abe."

Abe made a broad grimace. Linda looked confused. "It's an old saying," I told her. "I don't recall where I heard it."

*   *   *

The Brogardi rolled out on schedule and was, as expected, the movie of the year. While an onstage reconciliation between Abe and his father might have given us a burst of publicity, being able to sell "The Movie that Prevented a War!!!" was something that no other film could offer. If last summer marked the year of the Brogardi, this summer would celebrate the year of *The Brogardi*. Abe was hailed everywhere not only as an instant star, but as someone who had sacrificed himself in the cause of friendship for our two worlds. When news of his relationship with Linda broke, as was inevitable, that only added to his celebrity. No matter how many clarifications were issued by the Brogardi embassy, or how clearly Abe spoke in direct answer to interview questions, there were many who remained convinced that the real reason that ex-Ambassador Gezunt had nearly gone to war was because he was appalled that his son would fall in love with an Earth woman. So far as Abe or anyone else could figure out, his father hadn't even been aware of his relationship with Linda at the time. That didn't stop the tabloid writers, though, who compared Abe to King Edward VIII, who had sacrificed the throne of England for the woman he loved. Of course, Brogard didn't have royalty, and Abe had traded a dry academic career on Brogard for fame and fortune on Earth, but the romantic notion that Abe was a great lover who had sacrificed it all proved hard to contradict, especially since it helped to sell tickets to a movie that only served to reinforce it.

After several weeks, *The Brogardi* was closing in on box office gross of one billion dollars—and that was just the US and Canada—with no let-up in sight. I was sitting in my office, going over the release plans for our late summer films, when Junior summoned me for a sauna meeting. I think it was the privacy that he craved, more than the heat, since he and I had barely spoken more than two sentences to each other since that fateful morning in New York. Except for his appearance at the L.A. opening—including a party that was still going strong as the sun rose the next morning—he and Sylvie had been on an extended vacation. Unlike his usual holidays, this one had not involved peppering the folks back at the studio with memos and voice mail at each stop.

He was already lying on one of the benches, partially swathed in towels, when I entered the hot box. I took the ladle from the pail of water, and emptied a cupful of water on my head. The evaporation supposedly helped my pores open, or some such thing. All I knew was that it felt good, and since this was Junior's show, I was just to sit there until he told me why I had been summoned.

After several minutes of silence, and another ladling of water on my now steaming brow, I was beginning to wonder if he had fallen asleep. I cleared my throat, and when it got no immediate reaction, I did it again.

"You can hold the stage coughs," he said, without opening his eyes.

"Oh, hello Sly. I didn't know if you were awake," I said, innocently.

He turned around and sat up. He didn't look like a man whose stock portfolio had probably doubled or tripled in value in the last month, on the strength of *The Brogardi*. In fact, he looked terrible.

"Jake, I'm wondering if we did the right thing."

Hmm. That was a nice, general statement that could apply to almost anything. Even if I was a yes-man, which I wasn't, it was too soon to agree with him. The safest answer was the one I gave, "What do you mean?"

"With *The Brogardi*. I was so gung ho to be the first one out with a Brogardi star, that I never thought what it would do to him."

"Last time I spoke to Abe, he was pricing mansions in Bel Air and checking with medical and legal experts about the feasibility of making his relationship with Linda Reid permanent. I don't think he's complaining."

"But…"

"Further, he is being inundated with offers from every studio and independent producer in town. Do you know what he's telling them?"

"What?"

"To speak to you. He hired an agent who told him he was crazy, because he could make much more money elsewhere. He said he couldn't spend all the money he has now, and he fired the agent."

Sly seemed touched. He lifted one hand to his eyes, but I couldn't tell if it was to wipe away a tear or beads of sweat. I reached for the ladle again.

"And how is it affecting our relationship with Brogard? Have we created a star but ruined a friendship?"

"The new ambassador told the United Nations that everything was back on track, except that, for obvious reasons, now was not the time to start distributing Earth films and videos on Brogard. Abe is free to go home any time he wants to, and his mother is coming for a visit next month."

"And his father?"

"Life isn't like the movies, Sly. It may be a long, long time before they talk again. The Ambassador—I mean the ex-ambassador—is a stubborn man."

"Yeah, I liked that about him," he sighed. "What a shame."

"Meanwhile, Abe is something of a hero back on Brogard. I don't know how much you know about Brogardi affairs, but he's being hailed as someone who can adapt to new ways without sacrificing the old. There was a report in one Brogardi journal that he might run for office one day, although he said for now he's making his home on Earth."

"You read Brogardi?" I could have bluffed my way through and said yes, but Sly would have found me out sooner or later.

"No, I get it on their website. The Brogardi embassy provides numerous periodicals translated into several Earth languages."

"So Abe's happy, and—except for his father—Brogard's happy. I guess it turned out all right after all."

I must have let something show on my face, because Sly now sat up straight, once again the boss. "There's something you're not telling me."

"Well, I've been following how our film is being discussed in the Brogardi press, and that's where I found out about our piracy problem."

"Piracy?"

"There are illegal copies of *The Brogardi* circulating on Brogard."

"But how is that? They have no movie industry, no DVD players. How are they watching it?"

"Apparently, there's been some hardware developed to adapt Earth computers to Brogardi use, and vice versa, and someone has made a pirate version of the film that can be downloaded. It's all black market and very secretive. Even the writers of the articles claim only to have heard about someone who says that someone else showed it to them. Best I can tell, though, it seems to be for real."

"And what can we do about it?"

"According to Gretchen, not much. The Earth/Brogardi treaties deal with non-aggression and patents and civilian travel, but they kept putting off the copyright issues. Now we know why. Every bit of their non-fiction is considered to be in the public domain, and all of their fiction is deemed pornography."

Junior started to laugh. When he didn't share the joke, I asked, "What's so funny?"

"I'm sorry. But you know how Abe came to us, because we had the reputation for wholesome, family entertainment?"

"Yeah."

"Well, I'm now the biggest purveyor of smut on Brogard." Sly started to laugh again. "If my father was still alive, this would have killed him."

When I suggested what that would have meant on Brogard, we both started laughing even harder.

I hoped Larissa wasn't serving chicken tonight.

Epilogue
Journey to the Far Side of the Sun

Fourth of July weekend. *The Brogardi* had turned into the hit of the decade. People just couldn't get enough of this simple story. I believed it was really Abe they couldn't get enough of, but the film's good fortune had rubbed off on everybody. After years of being dismissed as Graham's "house director," Caroline was suddenly being invited to speak at film school seminars and getting profiled in film magazines. The famous Brattle Theater in Cambridge, Massachusetts, was planning a retrospective of her work. More important than the prestige was that she was now fielding offers from major production companies to commit to their projects, hoping that the "Sosniak magic" would rub off on them.

Perhaps most unexpected of all was the success of Irving Moskowitz. After the script was done, I had heard nothing more of him, which was not unusual given the generally low esteem with which writers are held in Hollywood. I assumed he had returned to whatever retirement home he had been living in when Junior put him back into harness. However, in mid-June *Variety* was reporting a fee in the high six figures for his next script. This had come about from a bidding war carefully arranged by his agent. The script about two friends, one Earthan, one Brogardi, who become pilots together and fall in love with the same woman, sounded awfully familiar to anyone who knew movie history—which was to say, of course, it was completely unknown to the young turks who were bidding on it. To make it interesting—and to further hype it to the skies—the script was delivered by armored truck to each of the bidders at 5 P.M. on a Friday, and they had until dawn of the following Monday to make their offers. My hat was off to whatever publicist had come up with that wacky scheme. I pointedly did not call Junior's office to see if we were among the loons fighting over this ancient chestnut.

We had invited some friends and family over for an Independence Day barbecue and swim, allowing Susie to greet each guest at the door and announce that her friend Abe was coming over this afternoon. The nice fallout from this was she recognized that it was her Dad—heretofore merely a flack for those kiddie "Ducklings" movies—who had brought Abe into the house and into our lives, thus making me a worthwhile member of the family again.

Abe brought Linda and his Uncle Behayma, who was visiting California for the first time, and we had invited several family members, including Larissa's parents and my cousin Norm. Norm and Behayma were deep into a discussion about which planet had benefitted more from the technological exchange, with each arguing that the other's planet was the more advanced. I told Rosa to water their drinks and otherwise leave them alone.

Larissa was in the pool with Elizabeth, who had celebrated her first birthday several weeks earlier, and was now twice as dangerous on two feet as she had been when she could only roll. In the wake of our near-tragedy last January, Larissa had embarked on swimming lessons for both the girls. I wondered what a baby could do in the pool, but Larissa turned out to be right: Elizabeth wasn't exactly Esther Williams, but she now splashed and kicked and otherwise had a great time in the water. That lack of fear was the most important thing she could learn at this age, so that as she got older, picking up more advanced techniques would be simple add-ons, rather than necessitate a psychological upheaval. Susie turned out to be part fish or, according to Abe, part Brogardi, gliding through the water above and below the surface as if it was her first home.

When Claire and Sidney arrived, I must have given a start, because my mother-in-law asked if I was all right. I suppose it was seeing Sidney, and wondering if it was really him, or Abe in disguise again. I realized I was being foolish. Abe no longer had to disguise himself as a human, although he was now working on a new version of *Dr. Jekyll and Mr. Hyde* in which he was going to be human as Hyde.

I was skeptical. "Isn't that going to make it look like humans represent the dark side of the Brogardi?"

"Actually, we're making it clear that there's a difference between the real humans and the one my character turns into. Hyde isn't a real human. He's a Brogardi nightmare version of one. We have a whole production number about that."

"Production number? You mean this is a musical?"

"Why not?"

"Well, can you sing?"

"I'm still trying to get the hang of the rhythms of your show tunes, but my coach says I'm coming along nicely. Remember, I was a music student on Brogard."

"You studied music, Abe. You didn't inflict it on others. Why don't you try something a little safer?"

"You mean like *Son of the Brogardi*?" He grimaced.

"You're taking a big chance," I said, as gently as I could. I'd seen too many careers skyrocket and then do fast fades.

"Why not take chances? With my percentage of the profits, I'll never have to worry about money again." He was right. *The Brogardi* had made so much money that even the monkey points were worth something. "That means that I'll probably never do another film which will be that successful, so why even bother to try? I want to try different things. Some will work, some won't. And if I wear out my welcome, I'm sure you can use your pull to get me into *The Ducklings' Brogardi Adventure*."

We had a good laugh over that. I saw Behayma making his way over to us, and after a few words, I excused myself to get some more ice. When I returned, they were talking about Abe's favorite hobby, unusual drinks. "It contains gin, dry vermouth, sweet vermouth, and Benedictine," Behayma told him. "It's called a Rolls Royce."

"Very interesting. I shall try to remember that one. By the way, did I tell you that I had Sex on the Beach?" Abe gave a good natured wheeze.

"Don't fall for that one, Behayma," I interrupted. "It's another drink. It contains orange juice, peach schnapps, vodka, and cranberry juice." I looked at Abe with satisfaction. "You thought you were going to put one over on us that time, didn't you?"

"I don't know what you're talking about, Jake. Linda and I went to Malibu last weekend, and watched the sun rise. Then we had sex on the beach. I'm glad we brought a blanket, it might have been very painful."

"Abe…" I said, wagging my finger.

"That drink sounds very tasty, though," he added quickly, "I must remember to try that one as well."

Behayma slapped the top of his head. "Oh, I almost forgot, your cousin Kuni is coming to Earth next month. He's going to be part of the new legation."

"Kuni is coming?" I saw Abe grin, showing several of his teeth. This was not good news. I didn't get it, until I remembered that this was his cousin the tattletale.

"Come on, Abe," I began, "we don't maintain childhood grudges on Earth—"

"Jake, you don't understand—"

"Actually, Abi, you're the one who doesn't understand," said Behayma. "One of the reasons he's coming is that he's become one of your most prominent defenders on Brogard. In fact, there are some who accuse him of being the one who's circulating your movie back home, but no one's been able to prove anything."

Abe seemed stunned. "Really?"

"Kuni is arguing that Earthan fictions"—he gave a small, nearly imperceptible wince as he said the word—"are really a form of truth. He's been pointing out how much we learned from the Earthan broadcasts, in spite of the fact that a goodly portion of them were false. He's being sent to make arrangements for limited access to Earthan movies, plays, and novels on Brogard, so that the citizens can engage in a more fully informed debate."

"Why, that's wonderful," said Abe.

Suddenly, I heard a shout from Norm. "Hey, everyone, look at this."

Norm and Sidney were in the living room, looking at the TV. The newsreader was intoning, "CNN has learned that Earth and Brogardi astronomers are both confirming that these signals are not coming from either planet. We repeat, these signals of unknown origin are coming from somewhere in deep space, and both Earth and Brogard have been ruled out as their sources."

"This is incredible," said Norm, "I've got to call JPL and find out what's going on."

Linda, Claire, and Larissa came in, followed by Abe and Behayma. Larissa held Elizabeth, bundled up in a towel after a vigorous swim, while Susan rushed to her side, allowing a chlorinated puddle to collect at her feet.

"Daddy, what's the man saying?"

"He's saying it's time to barbecue," I said, reaching for the remote and turning the set off.

"Hey," said Sid, "I was watching that. This is important news. This may mean Earth and Brogard are about to make first contact with a bunch of aliens."

Norm, one ear pressed to his cell phone, was similarly agitated. "Damn it, I can't get through. Jake, put the set back on. We might miss something."

I shook my head. "As we used to say when I was a kid: This is where we came in."

I herded everyone away from the TV and out onto the deck. Whoever it was that had come calling would just have to wait until tomorrow. As I started the fire, I had one last thought on the subject: Please don't let them be coming for Betty. She really is indispensable.

Acknowledgments

This book would not have been possible without the assistance of David Kaplan. When he learned that the computer files containing the manuscript had gone missing, and all I had was one printout which I was laboriously retyping, he introduced me to something called OCR: optical character recognition. According to David, this software would allow him to take my printout and transform it into a Word file. Well, he claimed it was software. Under Clarke's Third Law—that any sufficiently advanced technology is indistinguishable from magic—from my perspective he performed some wizardry. However it was done, thank you, David.

I also have to thank Michael Burstein and Lisa Ashton, early readers whose feedback and support was most helpful.

Of course everything here is fiction, but I have to offer my appreciation to two people who allowed me to engage in some borrowing. *Two on the Aisle*, the movie about the two film critics that pops up here, is an actual screenplay written by myself and Nat Segaloff. I thank Nat for letting me put it into production at Graham Studios. Anyone interested in putting it into production in *this* universe should contact Nat or myself.

Back in the 1970s, I was a busboy at the Raleigh Hotel in South Fallsburgh, New York, and got to see the Catskills before the resorts slipped into their final decline. The hotel no longer exists as such, but the night manager is played by my sister Bonnie—to whom this book is dedicated. Bonnie had several jobs there, including working behind the front desk. Her daughter's name really is Liza. I am proud to say that my niece did not shampoo the dog in the bathtub, but instead graduated from Sullivan Community College with high honors, and is now completing a course of study at Marist College. Thanks to both for their cameos here.

My mother, Rita, and my daughter, Amanda, are both happy that I'm finally publishing a novel after five works of non-fiction. While Abe's father back on Brogard would no doubt be shocked, this is the first of my books that they might actually read cover to cover. I hope they feel it was worth the wait.

Finally thanks to my agent, Alison Picard, for sticking with me all these years, and to my friend, editor, and publisher, Ian Randal Strock. It's been an interesting ride so far. Let's hope there's more fun in store on the journey ahead.

About the Author

Daniel M. Kimmel's film reviews appeared in the *Worcester Telegram and Gazette* for 25 years, and can now be found at Northshoremovies.net and SciFiMoviePage.com. He is local correspondent for *Variety*, the "Movie Maven" for the *Jewish Advocate*, and teaches film at Suffolk University. He writes on classic science fiction films for *Clarkesworld* and *Space and Time* magazines. His book on the history of FOX TV, *The Fourth Network* received the Cable Center Book Award. His other books include a history of DreamWorks, *The Dream Team*, and *I'll Have What She's Having: Behind the Scenes of the Great Romantic Comedies*. His collection of essays, *Jar Jar Binks Must Die... and other Observations about Science Fiction Movies*, was nominated for a Hugo Award for "Best Related Work." He is a past president of the Boston Society of Film Critics, and current co-chair of the Boston Online Film Critics Association. This is his first novel.